David Youngman
Runaway Missionary

"But Jonah rose up to flee unto Tarshish

from the presence of the LORD . . ." Jonah 1:3

by Randy Pilz

Hebrews 12:2

Paperback: ISBN-13:978-0-9971114-7-7
e-Book: ISBN-13:978-0-9971114-6-0

Boletus Media—Attalla, AL
2017

DEDICATION

To the late Pastor Robert C. Newman

Robert Newman pastored Faith Baptist Church in Winfield, IL for several years. It was the first Bible-believing church my mother, sister and I began regularly attending after my sister and I had each received Jesus Christ as Personal Savior in the early 1970's. The church slogan at that time was "The Church You've Been Looking For," and that proved true for us. Pastor Newman was a man called of God with an obvious Spiritual gift for shepherding people. Under his preaching and instruction, we each followed the Lord in Believer's Baptism and became members of that growing church. Within a year or two, Pastor Newman also personally led my brother Ron to salvation during a visit to the Newman's home.

Robert Newman was a keen student of history, particularly of Baptists in America, authoring the book *Baptists and the American Tradition* for our nation's bicentennial year. He would have appreciated and understood the historical setting of this novella. The last name of the character PASTOR BARNABAS NEWMAN was chosen in his honor because that fictional character shares the caring shepherd spirit of the real Pastor Newman.

DAVID YOUNGMAN: MISSIONARY RUNAWAY

Notes to the Reader

This work of fiction is based on themes taken from the Old Testament Book of Jonah in teaching God's mercy extends to all men, and that He is "not willing that any should perish" (II Peter 3:9). The story borrows many elements from Jonah but is not intended to be a complete retelling of that account.

The modern, preferred name identifying the aboriginal people of the territory which became the United States is *Native Americans*, but for hundreds of years the name used was *Indians*. That name appears in this story, based on history and the 1811 setting, without intended or implied prejudice toward any Native Americans.

CONTENTS

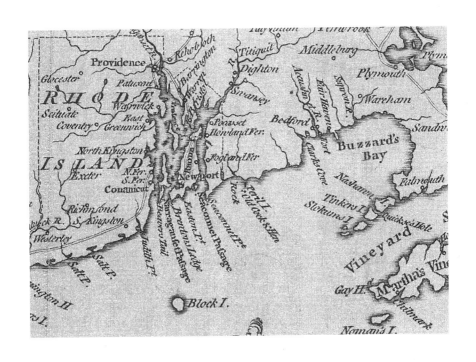

PROLOGUE

THE BRIG OF A BRITISH MAN O' WAR

The creaking of a wooden ship riding the waves. For some men, the sound, like joyful music, sings in harmony with the wind and the sea. But for one young man, the sound, like a monotonous dirge, drones-on in repeated groaning of a wretched beast that won't die—the discord of remorseful memories that continue haunting and tormenting his mind. Deep within the bowels of a British man o' war, bound in irons, the youth crouches in a dank hold, thinking with regret on the path his life has taken. A certain passage of Scripture comes to his mind, reminding him of the choices he's made: "Now the word of the LORD came unto Jonah the son of Amitai, saying, 'Arise, go to Nineveh, that great city, and cry against it; for their wickedness is come up before me.' But Jonah rose up to flee from the presence of the Lord."

Like Jonah, David Youngman has been running away. Away from God! At Christmas 1811, David Youngman has been running away, but now he squats in a foul-smelling brig, thinking on the bitterness of his life. Some men sin by loving what God hates, but David sinned by hating those God loves. His constant thought dwells on those choices leading him to this time and place.

A S.W. view of the COLLEGE in Providence, together with the PRESIDENT's HOUSE & GARDENS.

PART ONE: THE CALL

CHAPTER ONE

"I'll have nothing to do with Indians!"

BROWN UNIVERSITY

PROVIDENCE, RHODE ISLAND

AUTUMN 1811

David Youngman headed from University Hall back to his rented lodgings. The chill of a morning frost had given way to the glories of an Indian Summer afternoon on the campus of Brown University. David walked as he usually did, taking no notice of fat cattle grazing on pasture lands of the old Brown Farm stretching beyond the university. He walked along oblivious to the brilliant array of autumn leaves in the trees lining the nearby streets of Providence. He hung his head down, jammed his hands in his pockets. Keeping to himself: His goal, his purpose, his manner of life.

David kept to himself his first year at Brown. Continued his solitude into the second. He lived off-campus, boarding alone with a widow lady, a friend of his aunt. He avoided socializing with other students. Spoke in class only when called upon. On this particular afternoon something deflected David's protective shield of self-imposed isolation. His downward gaze came upon a pair of men's shoes belonging to a person standing directly in his path. The shoes neither shabby nor stylish, the practical kind often worn by tradesmen. The obstructing footwear forced David to prepare for interaction with a fellow student, a discomfort he avoided as much as possible.

David lifted his head. His upward tilting gaze followed the body of the shoes' wearer. David observed clothing a lot like his own dark gray outfit, save for the colors. He saw brown woolen stockings on a pair of skinny ankles; dark blue breeches on a pair of long legs; a tan woolen waistcoat with a white linen shirt beneath; a dark blue woolen jacket with three books tucked under the wearer's slender left arm; and a white stock tied at the high collar of his shirt. David's survey came upon a thin neck with prominent Adam's apple; a cleft chin; a smiling mouth; small nose; freckles across the cheeks and nose; clear blue eyes; and a mop of light brown wavy hair beneath a black, high-topped felt hat. The clothes fell shy of the cutting edge of fashion one saw in London or Paris, or even New York, but this was New England where tasteful expediency influenced men's wardrobes. The wearer's smile, friendly expression and extended right hand signaled an amiable situation void of conflict.

The person in his path, extending the hand, said, "Hello! Isn't this your second year at the university?"

"That's right," David answered, true as well as cautious.

The person extended his hand a bit further into David's personal zone. "I'm Theophilus Wilson. Seen you around, but never met you before."

"David Youngman, pleased to make your acquaintance," said David, as taught by his Aunt Abigail, looking the other young man square in the eye while taking the offered hand and shaking it. The hand felt warm and firm.

"My first name's a mouthful, sounds like a disease," the other young man laughed, "so folks call me 'Theo.' What are you studying?"

"History and philosophy, some natural science," David answered, keeping his answer unspecific, "as well as the standard languages."

"Ah, languages!" Theo flashed a delighted smile. "You're enjoying Dr. Newman's classes?"

"Yes, my favorites," David said. He wondered to himself how to bring this questioning to a polite conclusion.

"You should visit the little church Dr. Newman pastors sometime," Theo suggested. "You like his class, you'll love his sermons. A wonderful preacher."

David fended this proposition off with a noncommittal answer. "I'll keep that in mind."

"Assuming you're of a Bible-believing persuasion, will you be preparing for the ministry? Some of us are," said Theo.

"I don't think so," said David. How long these unpleasantries continue probing into his privacy? "I agreed to come here for two years. That may be all."

"Maybe you've heard, there's a group of us praying about missionary endeavors every Friday evening," said Theo. "Care to join us?"

David had overheard a little about this eccentric-sounding group. He didn't want to turn Theo down with point blank rudeness, so he gave a vague answer, "Maybe."

To David's inner dismay, this Theo seemed to take his noncommittal answer as an affirmative.

"The gathering's nothing fancy or formal," Theo rattled on. "Just some burdened students. We meet in a cowshed. Less than a mile off, beyond College Hill." He jerked his head toward the pasture land rising behind University Hall.

"Does the farmer know you're using his shed?" asked David. He had a genuine curiosity about that.

Theo laughed. "Yes. We've permission as long as we're mindful of our lantern and help him milk his cows if we've stayed all night. Most times we do."

"'Do' what?" David asked, not sure what Theo meant.

"Both 'stay all night' and 'help milk his cows.'"

"So you pray *through* the entire night?" David asked. He'd heard and uttered the usual simple prayers at meals and bedtimes. Brief extemporaneous prayers were offered by some of his professors before class. He'd endured verbose "Addresses to Divine Providence" by the long-winded pastor of his aunt's church over in Portsmouth. This kind of impromptu prayer—by a group of students, voluntarily meeting on a weekly basis, continuing all night long—something beyond his experience or imagination.

"Some can only stay for an hour or two," Theo continued, "but a few of us do greet the dawn."

"How do you continue in prayer without repetition?" David asked. "Surely you run out of things to pray for."

"Oh, no," Theo answered, laughing again. "Our prayers include thanksgiving and praise as well as supplications. Often we break out into a verse or two of a song. Our God is too marvelous for us to exhaust the worship due Him. And there's often too much for us to cover every specific request in one session, so we rotate our lists of petitions. This week we're praying for those overseas, for Dr. Carey's missionary and translation work in India, for example; for efforts on the coasts of Africa; and for those planting churches in Jamaica and the Bahamas."

"Do you ever pray for anything in our own country?" David asked.

"Certainly," said Theo. "We pray for complete abolition of the slave trade and the release of all remaining in bondage. I hope you're in favor of those petitions."

"Most heartily!" David said. Although the slave trade had made many Rhode Island ship owners, rum distillers and their investors rich, his own family had supported abolition and manumission since before the Revolution. He agreed with them on the issues, especially after seeing slavery firsthand while sailing down the coast in the company of his late uncle.

"Glad we're in agreement there." said Theo. "We're also praying for local, state and national leaders, for revival in existing local churches, and for missionary endeavors on our western frontier among the Indians."

Hurt fired anger within David. His eyes narrowed. "Did you say 'Indians?'"

"Well, yes," said Theo, taken aback, wondering how he had offended the new student. "There are efforts reaching Indians with the gospel."

"I'll have nothing to do with *Indians!*" David stormed off, almost knocking over another young man coming along the way to join them.

"But they need the gospel as much as any soul!" Theo called after David.

"That chap almost bowled me over!" said Robert Thacker, the young man coming to join David and Theo.

"I began telling him of our missionary prayer meeting," Theo explained. "He seemed interested 'til I mentioned efforts reaching the Indians. Hot-headed fellow!"

"What's his name?" Robert asked.

"David Youngman."

"Hmm. Heard he attended here last year and returned this autumn," Robert said. "Explains it."

"Explains what?" Theo asked.

"His reaction to Indians," Robert explained. "A Reverend *David Youngman* established a mission station reaching Indians beyond Lake Erie several years ago. A rival tribe raided their station. Massacred everyone except the reverend's seven-year-old son. The boy had hidden for days before help arrived."

"I remember hearing that story from somewhere," Theo said.

"This hot-head must be that lad. Namesake of his slain father, no less."

"I could almost see fires of anger flare from his eyes!" Theo said.

"We'll pray for him this weekend," Robert said, and the two young men walked off.

Back in the ship's hold, David rubs raw skin where leg irons chafed at his ankles while the pangs of conscience chafed at his soul. He remembers how God began working in his life.

When the following Sunday came, David rose earlier than usual. Still agitated from his encounter with Theo earlier in the week, he'd tossed and turned all night. Fitful slumber haunted again by dreams of his parents and the once-happy life he knew with them at their frontier mission station. The one-room cabin the Youngmans had lived in possessed few amenities, but it did have a wooden floor over a root cellar. They planted a vegetable garden, built a shed and paddock for livestock and constructed a low wooden platform under a brush arbor where David's father preached to Indians from a near-by village. A trader and his Indian wife ran a post about ten miles east, at the confluence of two rivers along the Greenville Treaty Line. The Army maintained a small wooden stockade, Ft. Vigilance, on high ground above the trading post. The nearest white settlers, a dozen families farming on warrant land, clustered by the fort and trading post. Few non-Indians lived west beyond the rivers and treaty line.

The Youngmans started their mission from a cabin near the trading post. They befriended Wissaketchak, a tribal chief. He desired more understanding of their message and invited them to move their station beyond the Treaty Line, closer to his villages. Risks overshadowed this open door, given the long-standing inter-tribal hostility and the recent Northwest Indian War. The area had remained peaceful since the Treaty of Fort Greenville five years before, but rumors of unrest hung like low clouds on the horizon. David's father ventured out, cleared land granted by the chief and moved the station and his family west. The relocation, planted in a spirit of trust, allowed the Youngmans greater access to the people. Friendships grew and bore the promise of spiritual fruit.

Life was pleasant for young Davy back then. Days found him running the woods with boys from the Indian villages. He learned their tongue, their food, their way of life. He joined in their games. His new-found friends joined him at meal times. Together they sat before his father, listening while he told them Bible stories and explained the way of salvation in Jesus Christ—a pleasant life for David indeed.

David recalled fleeting glimpses of the fateful morning when all that life ended in tragedy: *A dawn as red as the blood that would follow. A strange silence from the woods. Not a bird singing. No rustle of squirrels scampering through the leaves. His father, face pale, telling his mother to take Davy and wait down in the root cellar beneath their cabin. His father picking up a Bible, stepping from the cabin door, calling out words of friendship and peace, friendship and peace.*

His mother closing the outer door behind him, grabbing a water gourd carrying Davy down into the cool cellar and bundling him in a warm quilt. Being held close to her in the darkness. The feel of his mother's heart pounding. The smell of the earthen floor, the dried vegetables hanging overhead. Hearing his father's muffled shout, his mother's whispered prayers. Feeling her tears dropping onto his cheeks.

The waiting, waiting, waiting. Being left behind. Told to stay put, no matter what, until the hatch above opened up again. A hug. A kiss on his wet cheek. Looking up, seeing concern etched upon her face as she closed the hatch down over him. The sound of her dragging a rug and the table over the hatchway. More waiting. A far off scream. Another. More waiting. The floorboards creaking, many loud voices above, rough laughter. The table, tipping over, crashing above. Crockery smashing on the floor. Silence.

Waiting. Waiting. More waiting. Hours and hours in the darkness of the cellar. The water in the gourd running out. Pushing up at the hatch, but not budging the heavy weight above. Days it seemed, huddled, trapped in darkness. Fear, hunger and thirst gnawing at him.

Voices above. The table being dragged aside. Broken crockery scattering across the floor above as someone drew the carpet away. The trap door opening.

Light hurting eyes so long in darkness. Strange faces looking down. Grim faces. White men's faces. Soldiers from the fort. Being lifted from the cellar, taken into the yard before the cabin. Trying to drink water with painful swallows.

Two long holes being dug in the ground. Bodies lying face down beside them. Soldiers cover the heads and torsos with army blankets as David passes. Blood stained legs of his mother. A stained Bible near his father's bloody hand.

David shook himself from those raw images of what had been. Too restless to wait for his landlady to rise and prepare breakfast. He wrote her a polite note, slipped out, and saddled his horse. He rode through the streets of Providence, past darkened shops and houses as the morning sun rose behind him.

CHAPTER TWO

"Go right on in, sonny!"

A COUNTRY CHURCH WEST OF PROVIDENCE

SEPTEMBER 1811

David should have stayed back in Providence. He should have prepared himself for Sunday morning worship. But David directed his little bay horse through deserted streets and still slumbering homes toward rural expanses beyond.

Most students at the university attended services at the nearby First Baptist or one of the other churches in the city. The great Baptist Meeting House, still among the largest structures in New England, dominated the city skyline. The enormity of that church's congregation—a potential sea of prying strangers—made David uncomfortable. The hypocrisy of some in its membership, professing Christian brotherly love while still profiting from the slave trade, bothered him. The formality of some of the other local houses of worship constrained him as well. Too much like what he'd endured while living with his Aunt Abigail, his late father's sister, over in Portsmouth.

Not going to church at all could get David in trouble with college administrators if they knew. Instead of enjoying the pleasant sights and sounds of a delightful autumn ride in the country, he battled stirrings of conscience. Emotions swirled within his soul: Sorrow over his murdered parents; anger and hurt rekindled by Theo's comments about Indians; uneasiness about being at college; dissatisfaction with the churches back in Providence; and guilt about escaping into the farmlands outside of town. He dreaded having to lie, if confronted for his actions, as much as he dreaded having to bare his soul in explaining them. His internal tribulation resulted in self-inflicted, unrelenting misery.

In the early years after coming to live with his aunt and late uncle, when conflict within flared up, David could lose himself in playtime with his friend Marcus Trent. Marcus had hurts of his own to escape. He'd lost his parents during an outbreak of Bilious Fever. The kindred of loss bound the two boys in close comradeship. Both boys sought diversion through imaginary worlds. Sometimes they'd go into the fields and play at soldiering—stalwart "Sgt. Youngman and Sgt. Trent" of the Rhode Island Militia fighting the British at Bunker Hill or in the Battle of Rhode Island. Sometimes they'd go down to the waterfront. They'd lurk along the docks and piers, playing at pirating—the "Dreaded Twin Scourges of Narragansett Bay." Sometimes, with sticks for swords and Aunt Abigail's wide front porch for a castle, they'd play at being knights-errant—valiant "Sir David and Sir Marcus" rescuing fair damsels from dragons or ogres or other evils distressing the realm.

Sometimes the duo became a trio when Nancy joined in. "Little Nan," was Marcus' freckle-faced, pig-tailed younger sister. She tagged along when none of her own playmates came around. Little Nan had a clear crush on David in those days. Her infatuation irritated him. He fended her off, calling her names like "Prune-pit" and "Freckle Factory." But she craved his attention, so even his rudeness encouraged her. Sometimes Little Nan's presence so exasperated him that David and Marcus cruelly "ditched" her, running off too fast for her in skirts and petty coats to follow.

They'd welcomed Little Nan's full participation into their imaginary worlds only when they played at being knights. These times required a "damsel in distress." Other neighbor girls showed no regular interest, but Little Nan eagerly volunteered because of David. (But David made sure "Sir Marcus" always played the rescuer after the time fair "Princess Prune-pit" rewarded gallant "Sir David" by throwing her arms around his neck and planting an unwanted REAL KISS full on his unexpecting lips.)

In all their elaborate world of pretending, NEVER did the trio play about Indians on the warpath or an epidemic in the town—an unspoken understanding between David and Marcus and Nancy.

One glorious summer, David's uncle, Linus Claiborne, a prosperous merchant and bookseller, among other ventures, took the two boys along on a business voyage. They embarked aboard his chief trading schooner, the *Abigail*, named for his wife. David and Marcus sailed with Uncle Linus around to Boston, on up to Bangor, Bar Harbor, over to Halifax and back. On the way, they learned how to "hand, reef and steer" from real mariners. Marcus remained a "lubber" despite this instruction, but David took to it like a duck to water. He mastered different knots and the names and functions of each sail. In fair weather, he even took a hand at the helm. To their delight, Uncle Linus paid the lads 'cabin boy's wages' for their short voyage.

Their idyllic childhood days passed as an interlude, a brief shelter from the bitter winds of change. The trio separated after the elderly relatives caring for Marcus and Nancy in Portsmouth became infirm. More distant relations in Philadelphia took in Nan and Marcus. They arranged for her to learn the millinery trade. Marcus entered into an apprenticeship to a cobbler. David's education had been under private tutors, but his own life changes came. His uncle and aunt enrolled him in a Connecticut academy for his final college preparation.

David wrote and visited Marcus, but over the years contact between the two became sporadic and dropped off altogether as the young men because absorbed in their. Solitary David lost himself in his studies. He devoted pent-up energy toward Mathematics, French, Latin, and the rudiments of Classical Greek. He loved the Natural Sciences, having lived his first seven years in wilderness settlements. The recent discovery journeys of Lewis and Clark and Zebulon Pike fascinated him. He pored over their published reports, journals, sketches and maps. He would have enjoyed trekking overland into uncharted territory, as they did, and observing new terrain and new kinds of wildlife, except all of that would have also meant going west, into Indian lands, a thing he could NOT do.

David dragged his feet about entering college. He took a temporary appointment as a traveling secretary. Serving one of his uncle's merchant friends on a series of trading voyages, David enjoyed the anonymity the position provided. His journeys along the Eastern Seaboard lasted over a year.

David returned to Portsmouth still reluctant about enrolling in college. He toyed with the idea of accepting a clerical position in the diplomatic service and heading abroad when his kindly uncle passed away. Uncle Linus left a generous legacy to David in his will. There were stipulations: A liberal amount would become David's upon enrollment at Brown University, where Uncle Linus had been a trustee; further amounts would become David's upon completion of each year there. The balance became his upon graduation or after two years of college and five years in an established business. Seeing by this how much his college enrollment would have meant to his late uncle, David complied. He'd endured his first year at Brown and began his second, in honor of Uncle Linus more than thoughts about additional inheritance.

Entrance into the bustling university proved uncomfortable for David. Unlike his secretarial position, sheltered in shadows of obscurity, college life thrust him into the light of constant contact with strangers—those who didn't know and understand him and those who didn't care enough to leave him alone. He went to great lengths concealing his personal anger and anguish from outsiders.

David continued on his Sunday morning ride. His horse's hooves clomped over the river on John Brown's bridge. Cloaking himself with solitude, David passed by the neat rows of houses on the far side. He headed west, out the Arnold Road, away into farms and fields. His horse's hooves rustled along through fallen leaves along the way.

A couple of miles out, David turned down a lane bordered by trees and stone walls, lost in troubled thought. A sound penetrated his inner conflict. Something different out among these farms. Instead of birds twittering from hedges and orchards, cattle lowing in pastures or geese honking from a pond, David heard many voices united in joyful singing.

The lane brought him into a small crossroads hamlet. Less than a dozen sturdy cottages clustered together along the road. A tiny dry goods store, a blacksmith's workshop, a small tavern, and a grist mill with its waterwheel, stone dam and millpond rounded out the community. He'd passed through this rural settlement times before, heading to and from Connecticut. Back then, David hadn't noticed the little brown frame chapel perched on a green hillock behind the blacksmith. A grove of beech trees surrounded the hillock, which had screened the church building from view when in leaf.

The morning had turned warm. Perfect Indian Summer weather—although David avoided that expression and others with the word "Indian" in them. The doors and windows of the wooden church stood open. The singing he heard came from within. No liquor being served on Sunday, non-church-going idlers sat on the porch of the tavern enjoying the pleasant weather and spirited *a cappella* singing.

"Quite a concert going on across the way, sonny," called an old man to David from a bench on the tavern's porch.

David rode a few paces closer to the church and pulled up, listening again. The voices sang to the old Scottish hymn tune "Martyrdom."

"Go right on in, sonny! Been singin' up a storm. Haven't started the preach-afyin' yet." another man shouted. "Good preachin', too!"

Drawn by the hearty music, David crossed over into the grove, up closer to the church. Several farm carts and wagons, along with a few horses, belonging to the hamlet's "out-layers," stood under trees on the lower slope of the hill. David tethered his horse beside them. The beast swished his tail and began grazing on the thick grass. The people inside finished singing Isaac Watts' hymn "Alas, and Did My Savior Bleed?" and began Edward Perronet's "All Hail the Power of Jesus' Name" set to the tune "Miles Lane."

David thought to himself, *Whoever these country folk are, they're skilled in hymnody!* He trotted up the hill to the church. The rear of the building rested on the hill. Fieldstone pillars supported the front and sides because of the slope. A broad wooden stairway led up to the double-doored entrance. A couple of young mothers strolled about in front, walking their babies to sleep near the foot of the stairway and listening to the music. They nodded to him as he passed. He mounted the steps up to the open doorway two at a time.

Darker inside the building than out in the sunlight A few moments passed before David could discern the proceedings within. Desiring a better look, he took off his hat and stepped over the threshold into the back of the building. His eyes adjusted, and he could now see the church interior filled with people standing and singing. Their simple wooden pews arranged six or seven rows deep, with an aisle between—men and boys on one side and women and girls on the other, as some churches still practiced. Local farmers, most of the folk, he assumed by their clothing. Some of the men in the back wore working clothes and boots, coming straight from milking or caring for other stock.

A tall, smiling man stepped beside David, putting a firm, friendly arm around his shoulders. "Welcome, friend. Come on in," the man said. "A place right he-ah on the aisle."

The man guided David to a vacant spot three rows up from the back. David moved into the pew and stood beside the other men there as the song ended. A plain wooden pulpit stood at the front center of a raised platform. Four ladder-backed chairs lined the rear. No ornate crosses or stained glass windows adorned the building's interior, but a pleated maroon curtain hung across the wall behind the platform.

An enthusiastic young song leader stood behind the pulpit, leading the congregation in a clear tenor voice. David stiffened and gasped, recognizing the song leader—none other than Theo Wilson, the very student who'd triggered the flood of unpleasant memories and feelings driving David out by this place in the country!

David started to leave the pew, but Theo said, "Please be seated."

Turning back, David sat down with the other men. Exiting now, with everyone else seated, would expose him to unwanted stares, bring possible questions later. He waited. When they announced the next song, he'd slip back outside and hurry away.

"Thank you all for beautiful singing on a beautiful morning!" said Theo. His smiling rapport with the congregation showed a friendly and familiar relationship.

Probably working with the pastor of this church, David thought, *studying under him, gaining experience while preparing for the ministry, as he'd told me.*

"Robert will lead us now in prayer," said Theo.

Theo sat down on one of the chairs upon the platform as another young man stood and approached the pulpit. David thought he'd also seen him on campus but didn't recognize him as the student he'd almost knocked over in his abrupt exit from the conversation with Theo.

Surely too young to be the pastor, David thought. *Must be another student preparing for the ministry.*

While Robert led the congregation in prayer, David suppressed a strong urge to slip from the pew and bolt out of the church while others bowed their heads. Bowing his head, David peeked out below his eyebrows. He searched around for the pastor. Only one of the man's legs and part of his balding head were visible. The pulpit hid the rest of the man from view. Not much David could determine from the leg or head, except a man tall enough that the top part of his head, bushy eyebrows upward, was visible above the level of the pulpit's lectern while seated. A man probably up in years. The hair bordering the bald part of his head like a laurel wreath was gray at the back and side and white at the temple.

The men in the congregation murmured "Amen," as Robert ended his prayer and sat down beside Theo. David hoped for another song. He braced for a quick, quiet exit, but Theo kept his seat. The tall, balding pastor with the wreath of gray hair stood up beyond the pulpit and approached it.

Astonished David sank back in the pew. Of all the places of

worship in the Greater Providence area, it seemed Providence Himself had led David into the small country church pastored by Dr. Barnabas Newman, his languages professor at the college.

Dr. Newman paused before the people, smiled and took out his spectacles. He slipped these over his ears, adjusted them on the bridge of his nose. He smiled again, cleared his throat and began preaching in the strong baritone voice familiar to David from classroom lectures. "Beloved, I take for my text this morning these ten words from the Book of Isaiah, chapter fifty-three, *'He was a man of sorrows and acquainted with grief.'*"

Dr. Newman paused a moment, peering at his people over the top of his spectacles. He nodded ever so slightly and smiled, recognizing David among the men. Dr. Newman continued his address, repeating the text, *"He was a man of sorrows and acquainted with grief.'* Thus Isaiah spoke of Jesus Christ centuries before our Savior walked this earth, yet the Holy Spirit moved Isaiah to accurately describe Jesus in both His humanity and His deity.

"Our Lord Jesus knew the pain of loss. Rejected by His fiends, His family, His nation. While Jesus Christ is high and lifted up, Very God of Very God—the Almighty—He's not a dispassionate observer. He's not one who sits back in Heaven, coldly watching us wallow in trials, tribulation, disease and distress on earth below. Jesus Christ is also *Immanuel.* That name means 'God With Us,' the One fully knowing, fully understanding from experience, the sorrow and grief, the painful tragedy of human existence. Jesus is the One standing beside us in that pain. He is the both the One who pronounced the curse on Fallen Man and is the One who fully tasted the bitterness of that curse Himself, on our behalf.

"Jesus Christ not only feels our pains but brings us the remedy, relief, release, redemption and restoration we need. He brings *'healing in His wings,'* as the Psalmist says. He is the One who sweetened the bitter waters at Meribah. The One who can give *'beauty for ashes.'* The One who says, *'Take my yoke upon you . . . and ye shall find rest for your souls . . . for my yoke is easy and my burden is light.'*"

David leaned forward in his pew, focusing on Pastor Newman's heartfelt discourse. Scripture after Scripture unfolded before him. The message that Jesus cares for him, feels with him, filtered through the hurts and sorrows of David's life and resounded within. As if Pastor Newman possessed intimate knowledge of David's inner pain this past week and prepared this message just for him. The theme brought remarkable refreshment in David's spirit and quieting of his anger. The encouraging words so uplifted him that he easily endured the hearty greetings of the curious church folk afterward and conversation with Theo, Robert and Dr. Newman during lunch that followed.

From that weekend onward, David attended Pastor Newman's church. The congregation followed a Sunday schedule typical of many country churches: two daytime services with a meal on the grounds in between. David would rise early, pack a couple of textbooks to study and some prepared food to share. He'd ride out and spend the day, returning to his boarding house with the setting sun.

David had experienced sporadic spiritual growth up to this point. The aloof, formal pastor at his aunt's church back in Portsmouth had been selected years ago for prestige his family connections brought the church. That somber man read his dull sermons in dull tones. Those dry bones offered little spiritual nourishment or doctrinal sustenance, more conducive for sleep than for Christian growth. A refreshing contrast, Pastor Newman used no written manuscript and few notes. He opened his Bible and preached unrehearsed from a true shepherd's heart in a compelling, personal way. His stirring messages fed milk and meat and honey to David's hungry soul. David's heart softened. A desire to live closer to God awakened within.

CHAPTER THREE

"Unattached and unaffected now because of a single-minded devotion to God"

AROUND PROVIDENCE

OCTOBER 1811

The revival in David's spiritual life brought an unexpected side benefit, a pleasant and surprising one. It came the third weekend in October during a visit by David's childhood friend, Marcus. Marcus had completed his apprenticeship and returned to the island. He now worked for an established cobbler down in Newport, making and mending footwear for townsfolk, farmers, sailors and fishermen. Plying this busy trade sometimes brought Marcus sailing up to Providence with the master cobbler for buying leather from local tanners and other supplies. During these brief trips, Marcus and David had renewed their friendship.

Previous visits, Marcus and David had sometimes shared a meal, but the needs of the master cobbler limited their time together. Now Marcus was making a buying trip on his own. He planned this next business visit so he could spend ample time with David. Marcus wrote that he was also bringing a surprise with him when he came. David wondered what the surprise might be. Maybe a pair of shoes or boots made especially for him by Marcus.

Haggling with the tanners occupied Marcus' attention on Friday and through Saturday morning. David and Marcus arranged for a lunch meeting on that day and for spending the afternoon and all day together on Sunday before Marcus sailed back down on Monday morning. David desired to show Marcus the college and especially his new church home out in the country.

Late Saturday morning, David walked down toward the waterfront inn where Marcus lodged. On his way, he passed residents of Providence out shopping or walking in the autumn sunshine. He kept to himself, tipping his hat or nodding a greeting where obligatory. He avoided making more than brief eye contact, whereever possible, especially with young ladies out and about. Conversations with these inevitably left him feeling awkward, tongue-tied and led to subtle, probing personal inquiries. Brown University enrolled an all-male student body, so David rarely encountered females around his age except when out in the city of Providence itself or at the country church. His self-imposed isolation limited those encounters on purpose.

David came around a street corner, heading toward the inn. He noticed a young lady ahead of him. She strolled along carrying some packages wrapped in paper and secured with twine. *Been out shopping,* David thought.

David's avoidance of young women didn't negate an attraction to, or appreciation of, feminine pulchritude. His solitude enhanced their mystique to some extent. From his safe vantage point behind the young lady, he admired chestnut curls of her hair dangling beneath her stylish bonnet, pleasing symmetry of her face whenever she turned her head, gentle curve of her eyebrows, shape of her nose, her smooth cheeks and full lips.

Attractive girl. Wonder who she is? David mused. He marveled at both the pretty girl and these uncharacteristic thoughts flowing through his own mind. Something about her seemed familiar, but he couldn't put a finger on it. Not one of the girls from the country church. Only a handful there of her age still single or unspoken for. Those hardy farm girls either shorter or stouter than the slender young maid gracing the walkways here. Not a refined city girl among the gaggle in the great Baptist Meeting House here in town, either— he'd surely remember one as attention-grabbing as this—yet something intuitive triggered deep within. Couldn't shake the impression he that knew her from somewhere.

The young lady with the packages continued walking along in the same direction as David himself, oblivious to his prolonged observation. David appreciated the grace of her movement, the tasteful reserve of her blue street suit and the enchanting soft swish of its broadcloth.

The fascinating young miss crossed the street toward the very inn and tavern where David headed. Absorbed in espionage, he stepped into the street after the comely lass without checking for traffic. He almost collided with draft horses and a heavy wagon bearing down on him. The teamster, also distracted by the fetching maid crossing over before him, roused back to attention when one of his big horses reared up because of David's intrusion. He hissed a gruff rebuke at David.

The wagon rolled on by, blocking David's view. He hoped the girl hadn't noticed the near accident and coarse reprimand his gaffe incurred. When the wagon moved away, David trotted across and beheld the young lady approaching the doorway of the inn. He came up to her as she tried managing the door with all her bundles. One package slipped from her gloved hand and tumbled down by her feet.

David stepped in, picking up the package and helping her with the door. "Please allow me, ma'am." Their eyes meet, held for a breathless moment. David swallowed hard. The girl's red lips parted with a soft gasp of surprise. She smiled at him. An electric thrill raced through David. She took the package from David, and tilted her head with a questioning expression in her blue eyes. "Thank you, kind sir."

"Your servant, ma'am," David said, blushing, removing his hat. He fumbled with the handle, pulling the door open further while she entered. He dropped his hat. The young lady chuckled softly to herself as she passed, amused by some private joke. David picked up his hat and followed behind. He stood in the common room watching as she ascend the stairway. She turned at the top, smiled and nodded toward him. David dropped his hat again. His pulse raced from this friendly female attention. He bowed in return, eyes glued upon her as she moved away down an upper hallway.

Someone nudged David's elbow, breaking the enchantment. He discovered Marcus beside him, laughing. "Well, well, Davy! I see you discovered my surprise!"

"Marcus!" Davy hugged him. "What? What is your surprise?"

Marcus gestured to the hallway above. "You helped her through the door and gawked at her up the stairs!"

"Well, well, yourself! You didn't tell me you had a sweetheart," David said, picking up his hat. "Quite a lovely girl! You're very lucky."

"A sweetheart for someone some day, but not me." Marcus laughed and jerked his head toward the stairway. "Surely you know who that is, don't you?' Marcus shook his head in disbelief. He grabbed David by the shoulders and shook him gently. "You really didn't recognize her?"

"Well, something about her seems familiar, but I followed her here for the last ten minutes wracking my brain trying to figure out the connection. I must say, she's one of the most appealing young females I've ever seen around Providence," David said. "I don't talk about girls much, but she's exceptional if you ask my opinion."

"The opinion of many young men from Philadelphia to Newport and points in between," Marcus said.

"You know her? Wish I did. May I be introduced?"

"Of course I know her!" Marcus paused, staring David a moment, still incredulous that David hadn't caught on. "Davy, you know her too! No introduction necessary. That's *Nancy*! You didn't recognize my little sister Nan, 'Princess Prune Pit,' our old damsel in distress?"

"Nancy?! Her?!" David's mouth hung open. He hadn't recognized her, but she'd recognized him—her questioning look and her amused chuckle at his dumbfounded reaction when helping her through the door. *Nancy!* Seen again for the first time in years. Seen again but with different eyes. She'd metamorphosed from a gawky caterpillar into a graceful butterfly. Nancy! The irritating little freckle-faced tag-along had grown up. No wonder she'd chuckled at him. The tables had turned on David—he'd been tagging along today!

"Told you a few months ago how she'd returned from Philadelphia. Brought her along today so she could buy some craft supplies," Marcus explained. "Ribbons, feathers, dew-dads and such. She's quite a hat and bonnet decorator now. Orders coming in for her millinery creations from finer shops in Newport, here in Providence and over in Hartford."

"She has a particular male friend?" David asked. He braced himself for the affirmative.

"Oh, no!" Marcus chuckled. "Not now."

Davy felt surprising relief with that answer.

"No amount of flattery or flirting can win her favor anymore," Marcus continued with a shake of his head. "Unattached and unaffected now because of a single-minded devotion to God, of all things!"

"Devotion to God?"

"Puts a damper on a young feller's fervor, that's for sure! It's why she's returned to the island. Could've had her pick of Philadelphia suitors, but best if she explains all that herself."

Nancy reappeared at the top of the stairs. David smiled up at her, she smiled back and came down the stairs. She reached out and took David's hands in greeting and gave him a brief hug. All three laughed over David's failure to recognize her. They retired to a table for lunch.

The trio had a lot of catching up to do. Marcus and Nancy told of their current situations and working at both of their crafts around Newport. Marcus lodged over the master cobbler's workshop in the town. He often labored at his workbench from dawn to dusk. Nancy lived out at their grandparents' farm. Her grandfather converted part of a shed into a workshop for her. Other than church activities, she kept to herself. She'd found contentment in her work and in the quiet times she spent with God.

"I tell her she's become a Baptist nun," Marcus teased.

"Acts 20:24 begins, 'But *none* of these things move me, neither count I my life dear unto myself, so that I might finish my course with joy,'" Nancy quoted. "That's the only kind of 'none' for me."

David nodded to her in agreement. At first, he struggled being in her presence. Nancy's kindness and patience overcame his tongue-tied self-consciousness. Bonds of friendship renewed from childhood days. He opened up and shared about his college experience and about the new church home he'd found out in the country.

The spiritual transformation in David since attending the country church struck a chord with Nancy. She opened up as well, confessing details about the shallow and self-centered lie she'd lived as a carefree coquette back in Philadelphia. She'd led along a string of beaus, moved among finer social circles and reveled in the attention she received. A year ago, revival among the people at her church revealed her lost spiritual condition. She faced a difficult point of decision, continue in sin or commit her soul to the Savior. She chose Jesus Christ. Her trust in Him turned her away from her proud, flirtatious past. She avoided the callow young men she once attracted, determined now to live for God. Breaking from the pull of her old ways, she returned to Rhode Island. She now lived a quieter, more fulfilling life and found joy in serving her Lord.

Later, Nancy wrote an uncharacteristically long entry about her weekend visit to Providence in her diary:

Returned today from the buying trip up to Providence with Marcus. Almost didn't come along, but Marcus insisted, saying he'd arranged a surprise for me. So glad now I came!

Friday, Marcus took care of his leather buying, while I ordered supplies for hats and bonnets. Saturday morning, I picked up the orders and headed back to our lodging. At the door of the inn, I encountered Davy Youngman again, the first time in over six years. Not the same old Davy! Not just taller and a striking young man on the outside—the Lord has been changing him in wonderful ways on the inside!

We hired a carriage. Davy took us all around town, showing us the sights—the great Baptist Meeting House, the University, the Providence State House and the fine homes on College Hill. He even showed us a quaint little cowshed where students meet to pray. A pleasant dinner followed with a walk along the seashore and a breath-taking sunset on our way back to the inn.

Sunday, we rose early and drove our carriage out to a wonderful little country church Davy's been attending. Marvelous singing by those farm families and dynamic preaching there by Dr. Newman, one of Davy's university instructors.

Pleasant hours flew by during our visit. We spent most of the remaining time talking together, not the usual fluff I used to enjoy from the Philadelphia and Newport boys. A great blessing hearing from Davy about Christ working in his heart and a growing desire now to serve Him!

This morning, Davy showed up at dawn and saw us onto the boat before he hurried off to class. Told me, "I really enjoyed time together with you. Wish it could go on and on." Made me feel so good! Squeezed his hand and said seeing him again was "an unexpected blessing!" He asked permission to write to me. Told him, "Yes! Please write. I very much want to hear more of God's leading in your life. And I shall write back and tell of His leading in mine." Then I added, "If you ever come down to Newport, please call on me." Never thought I'd be telling any young man that sort of thing again! But this time felt the freedom to do so.

Strangely sad when our boat sailed away from the dock. Davy stood waving, as did I, until lost from view. Marcus teased me for my tears, but I don't care! Hope Davy writes to me soon!

Before departing back to Newport, Marcus told David in private, "Surprising, the way Nan's opened up to you. She doesn't pay more than polite attention to gentlemen callers these days. Keeps them all at a distance. Some who followed after her from Philadelphia went away calling her 'The Stubborn Rose of Newport.' Simply amazing!"

"Amazed myself," David said. "An awful time talking with girls before, but Nan's different. Telling her all the things the Lord's been doing in my life this semester came easily. Her interest made the words flow. Think she may still like me a little?"

"A little?" Marcus laughed. "The 'Stubborn Rose' comes into bloom again!"

"Wait a minute! Don't go thinking anything between us more than being old friends. It's *Nan*, after all, almost like she's my little sister too."

"I think you've seen she's not so 'little' anymore," Marcus said. "Told both of you I had a surprise waiting, but what a surprise for me, the way this weekend's turned out!"

All through the remainder of the fall term, boats sailing up and down Narragansett Bay carried letters between David and Nancy. Knowing the other understood past pains and backgrounds gave each of them liberty in expression. Drawing closer to God drew them closer to each other. He found putting thoughts and feelings down on paper cathartic. No other young men, until now, had shown the kindred spirit in the Lord that Nancy craved for in fellowship. She found joy in sharing her heart with David and what she learned from Scripture. She treasured his respect for her desire to put Christ first in everything.

Jonah 1:1a *"Now the word of the LORD*

came unto Jonah the son of Amittai . . ."

CHAPTER FOUR

"Brother David, is God calling you?"

A FARMER'S SHED BEYOND COLLEGE HILL

EARLY DECEMBER 1811

All through the remaining weeks of the term, fellow students prayed for David. They did not want to shoo him away with over enthusiasm, but kept up a gentle urging for him to join with them in their Friday evening prayer time. Nancy had also encouraged him to attend. He didn't want to go merely as an act, attempting to impress her or others with false piety. Just before the Christmas recess, he said he would attend the final meeting of that term and see for himself what happened there.

David rode over College Hill and out to the farm beyond. The cool evening air carried a hint of approaching snow. He entered the cowshed into the welcome glow of a lantern, the sweet smell of the hay and a warm greeting from Theo and Robert and the dozen other young men gathered there. The gentle cows added to the peaceful atmosphere.

"Glad you're finally joining us, David," said Theo. "Find a

comfortable spot."

"But not too comfortable," Robert said, "if you're prone to nodding off like Benjamin here did during the Rhetorical Ethics lecture last Monday."

"Hey!" protested the young man named Benjamin. "Mondays are hard! I'll do better tonight."

"We can tease Benjamin later," Theo said. "Important business lies before us. Brethren, let us pray!"

Some of the men knelt in the hay, most sat, and Benjamin remained standing so he wouldn't fall asleep. David found a place near the door while the others bowed their heads in prayer. The small group prayed with power and conviction. At intervals, one would begin singing, and the rest would join in. Hours went by. Tentative at first, David yielded his own heart bit by bit and joined with the others in their spirit of concern for lost men and women at home and abroad.

Dawn approached. David scarcely noticed the time passing. The earnest prayers continued.

"Merciful Savior,' Benjamin prayed now, "millions of souls need to hear the good news of salvation through faith in Jesus Christ. We pray Thou wilt raise up new missionary endeavors. Lord of the Harvest, send forth laborers into Thy harvest seeking souls to be saved."

Some of the others murmured "amen" in agreement. A long time since David had been among those with such a clear burden for the gospel. The praying students' commitment to Jesus Christ brought back smothered memories of his father and mother's zeal for their Savior.

"The same way Thou didst set apart Barnabas and Saul to be the first missionaries," Benjamin continued, "we pray Thee, choose from among us those Thou wouldst set apart and send out in this present day."

Another murmur of "Amen" from the others.

While the college men prayed, God began answering their prayer.

David raised his face toward heaven, experiencing something new and powerful. Not from emotion, nor from logical reasoning. Jesus' words "*Pray ye the Lord of the Harvest that He send forth laborers into His harvest*" echoed deep within David's soul. An unshakable conviction crystallized within, like a diamond—firm, sharp and dazzling clear: He knew God called *him*—David Youngman—as a gospel-bearing missionary!

As David pondered this certainty, the Holy Spirit also began dealing with him about the hatred he fostered in his heart.

"Call one of us, Lord. Send him to the shores of Africa, distant Asia or even among the native tribes here in America," prayed Benjamin. He prayed from his Spirit-led heart without malice. David's past had not entered his thoughts. Indeed, of those praying, Benjamin knew the least about David, but he did know of the great spiritual need in every corner of the world.

A murmur of agreement again. Inner peace melted away. David glanced up from prayer in horror. He bowed his head once more, but agitation kept growing. He could not remain still.

"Send him to those Indians who walk in the darkness of sin and most urgently need the good news of salvation in Christ," Benjamin continued.

David trembled, fighting the conviction of those words. He struggled within his heart, reaching for the love of Christ toward others while still clutching hatred for the Indians who killed his parents, but he couldn't hold both. His uneasiness intensified. He battled in his soul, dreading where God's call led him.

David stood up. The onslaught of conviction overwhelmed him. He blurted out, "No, Lord! I cannot!"

The others stopped praying. The shed stood silent. A cow shifted its weight. Theo asked, "David, what is the matter?"

David yelled up at God, in defiance of the unacceptable, "I

will not!"

"Brother David, is God calling you?" Robert asked. He moved over and put a gentle hand on David's arm, to calm him.

"Let me go!" David jerked his arm away. He shoved the door open and ran from the building. Yanking the reins loose, he mounted his horse. Heels dug into the startled animal's ribs, and the beast and rider galloped off into the cold darkness.

The men inside the shed paused in shock. The farmer's dogs barked at the pounding of horse's hooves fading away.

"Let us pray for our brother, David," Robert finally said. He pulled the door closed again, and the group settled back into prayer, interceding on David's behalf.

The bowels of the warship feel cold and damp. Cut off from light and fresh air, they stink of mildew, bilge water, and the staleness of humanity, but David barely notices. He directs his thoughts leagues away, mulling over the days since he ran from that prayer meeting.

Jonah 1:3a *"But Jonah rose up to flee*

from the presence of the Lord . . ."

CHAPTER FIVE

"There's war in here, Marcus. I can't explain, but I must go."

A HARBORSIDE TAVERN

NEWPORT, RHODE ISLAND

MID-DECEMBER 1811

David kept to himself the few remaining days of the term. He refused to talk about the prayer meeting and determined not return to the university after Christmas. No rest for him there, only reminders of the call of God, conviction he dreaded and confrontation with those who had prayed that night. Without telling anyone, he planned escape, running as far as he could get away.

David returned to Portsmouth, but he told Aunt Abigail nothing of the prayer meeting or of his plans. Christmas drew near, only a few days off. A blanket of fresh snow covered the island town. A festive, holiday spirit filled the townspeople. This irritated David all the more and fueled his desire to leave.

David rode his horse down the island to Newport. He told his aunt he wanted to see Marcus. That lie covered his plans on going to the harbor seeking a ship to take him away. He ran into Marcus on the way to the waterfront.

'Davy, what are you doing here?' Marcus said. "We thought you were still off at college!"

"It's Christmas recess now," all David said.

"Your Aunt Abigail must be glad to have you home for a while," Marcus chattered on. "What brings you down here? Come calling on Nan? She'll be so happy to see you."

The end of the fall term and return to Aunt Abigail's for Christmas had brought the flow of letters to a halt. In all his selfish, hasty plans to run away, David had only vaguely considered Nancy in any of them. New pangs of conscience struck his heart. He thought, *How in the world do I explain to her what I'm doing?*

"Quite a correspondence going on!" Marcus teased. "Nan talks about you all the time."

"Well, I'm not here looking for your sister," David said. "I'm looking for a ship. I'm going away."

"Going away?! What about the university?"

"I'm going to Paris," David said. "There are great universities in France. I'll study history and philosophy there."

This sudden reversal in David perplexed Marcus. He liked the new David of past October better. "And what about Nancy?"

"I'll continue to write to her, perhaps," David said.

"But why leave now?" Marcus asked. "Christmas is almost here. Bad sailing weather, too. There's war in Europe!"

David pointed to his heart. "There's war in here, Marcus. I can't explain, but I must go."

"Does your aunt know?"

"No, not yet," David said. "Haven't come up with a way to tell her. The least she knows the better. The same thing with Nancy.

34

First I must find a ship." A thought came to him. "Come with me, Marcus, and see the world!"

"I'm stuck in dull little life and would love a change," Marcus said, "but I'm no scholar, just a cobbler. How'd I survive in Paris?"

"They wear shoes in France," David reasoned. "You can be a cobbler there just like you are here. You're free to leave?"

"I guess so," Marcus said. "My apprenticeship's completed. I have only a handshake agreement with the cobbler I work for. Boarded here in town, but I'm staying out on my grandparents' farm now for the holidays. What will we do for money? You thinking of us working our way across?"

"No. I'll pay your passage," Davy said. "I have part of the money remaining from the legacy my uncle left me. There's more than enough for both of us. Come on, maybe there'll be sailors in this tavern who'll know of ships sailing east."

They entered a large harborside tavern. Inside the establishment smelled of tobacco, coffee, and onion stew. A smoky haze hung in the air. The pair glanced around, their eyes adjusting to the dimmer light. They noticed a friendly-looking old salt relaxing by the hearth and approached him. The sailor tipped his chair back on two legs, leaning against the wall. The mariner sized up the young pair, puffed on his pipe and nodded a friendly greeting.

"Excuse me, sir," said David. "Would you know of any ships headed soon for Europe?"

"Well, me lads," began the sailor, "used to be a few at this time of year, though winter storms be a-brewin', but now there be even fewer willin' to chance passage with the British a-watching those bound for the Frenchman's coast. Not me, for sure."

"The blockade?" David asked.

"But we have no part in their wars," added Marcus.

"See now, England's almost alone a-struggling with Bonaparte," the sailor explained, "and the Royal Navy wants none a-

35

trading in his ports. Few will venture there now, but I know of one captain. Run their blockade several times, he has. He's wily or a fool, but his risks have made him quite rich. Might be a-sailin' soon to France, the way his ship's all loaded down. Hasseltine's his name, Captain Hasseltine. Sits in yon corner. Comes to business, he be a right shrewd man. Make it worth his while, he'll be a-takin' you."

"Thank you," said David. "We'll talk with him."

The sailor pulled out his pipe and pointed the stem at the pair. "Be a-warnin' you lads! Rumors whisperin' about a British frigate off this coast right now, a-waitin' to catch Hasseltine. If you're stopped, you be a-risking' impressment!"

"Impressment?" Marcus asked.

"Not always contraband the British be after," the sailor explained. "They want men too. Been a long fight with old Boney-part. Manpower's scarce in Britain. The Royal Navy stops American ships on the high seas a-searchin' for British subjects, or those they claim to be British, forcin' them into their Navy." He gestured, showing a tiny distance between his thumb and forefinger. "Came this close to gettin' me, back in '09, and I won't let 'em have chance at me again."

"They just can't force a man," said David.

"That's kidnapping!" said Marcus. "Like slavery!"

"Aye, worse than slavery! But when they be openin' their gun ports and a-runnin' the cannon out, 'tis a strong argument they have," said the sailor.

"Thank you for the information and the warning," David said.

Moving away from the sailor, David said, "I'm still going away, Marcus, whatever the risk. I must get far away!"

"I'm not so sure, Davy," said Marcus. "I don't like what he said about the blockade."

"I must go!" David insisted. "Let's see what this Captain Hasseltine has to say." The young men crossed the room. The man they assumed to be the captain sat alone at a corner table. The short, husky man wore a bridge coat with shiny brass buttons. He'd finished his stew and drank from a steaming mug of coffee.

"Excuse us, Captain Hasseltine, may we speak with you a moment, sir?" David asked.

"Yes, my lads, how may I help you?" said the captain.

David lowered his voice. "Someone said you might sail soon to France,"

"What gave him that idea?" asked the captain in an equally lowered voice, his eyes narrowing in suspicion.

"He said you've done so before," David explained.

"And your ship seems all loaded down and ready to sail," added Marcus.

Captain Hasseltine looked the pair over with a cautious eye. "Maybe and maybe not. Suppose my ship's preparing to sail, just *supposing*. Do you have cargo or are you looking to go to sea yourselves?"

"We would book passage," David said. "If such passage is available."

The captain lifted his mug and sipped from it, considering what David said. He set down the mug. "When I sail, I usually take a few passengers, but the present European situation has made such travel, um, 'unattractive' as of late."

"You're talking of the blockade?"

Hasseltine gestured for the pair to come closer. "Have a seat, my lads." He kept his voice low and leaned across the table. His eyes narrowed, taking on an expression of sagacity. "Some risks are worth running, my young friends, if the profit's high enough. That's my credo. I've a fast ship and a load of rice from the Carolinas. I'll risk sailing through storms and under the noses of the British navy, if need be, because this cargo will bring an enormous profit mid-winter in Bordeaux." He paused, letting all that sink in. "Sail with me, if you dare!"

"Rumors say a frigate might be lurking out there waiting to catch you," Marcus said.

The captain gave a hearty laugh. "Rumors! There's always rumors, lads! Small chance there's a frigate's off this coast in winter, but I've got fishermen and whalers watching for me. Only a slight risk."

David and Marcus exchanged glances.

The sea captain leaned back in his chair. "If you come, you must pay for your passage and double the usual rate. I've no need of extra crew."

David showed him his money pouch. "I have this."

Hasseltine weighed the purse in his hand before passing it back, "Ah! A fat enough purse!"

"When will you set sail, if you do?" David asked.

Hasseltine lowered his voice again and glanced around once more. "I may up anchor at dawn on Christmas Day. My ship's the *Pocassett*. Be at the dock with your money by sun-up that morning, if you're coming. I'll keep berths open for you." His eyes darted around the room. "But don't tell anyone!"

CHAPTER SIX

"Who knows what the cost may be if your Heavenly Father must reach out in love and chasten you back to Himself?"

AUNT ABIGAIL'S HOUSE

PORTSMOUTH, RHODE ISLAND

DECEMBER 1811

The fires of conviction slowly subsided within David's soul as he planned for a different life far away. Only a few embers troubled him, but on Christmas Eve they flared up again and burned hot indeed!

Christmas bells decorating the front door jingled again as the front door opened. "Merry Christmas, Abigail! Thank you for inviting me," said a voice from the foyer.

Another Christmas Eve guest had arrived. Down the hall in his room, David had heard each of the others arrive. His aunt and late uncle observed a long-standing tradition of dinner and an evening with close friends to ring in the holiday. David kept to himself as much as politely possible but hurried out to help the servant girl with each new arrivals' coats, hats, and shawls.

"Merry Christmas to you, Barnabas!" said Aunt Abigail. "You're very welcome. I'm so glad you could come! Davy, please come and help Pastor Newman with his overcoat."

David already approached but stopped short when he saw the last arrival. There stood one of the people David sought most to evade, kindly Pastor Barnabas Newman.

Aunt Abigail passed David in the hall. "Auntie, you didn't tell me Dr. Newman was coming!" said David, hiding his anxiety in a voice above a whisper.

Aunt Abigail laughed merrily. "Davy, you look so shocked! Do you know Dr. Newman?"

"He's my languages professor at the University. I've attended his church most of the semester."

"Well, how wonderful!" Aunt Abigail laughed again. "Having him come is a last minute thing, but he's a dear old friend. Hasn't visited here since before your uncle died. Put his things in the guest bedroom, please. He'll be staying over Christmas."

"Staying?!" David asked, but Aunt Abigail had moved on. Those gathered in the big front parlor applauded when she announced Dr. Newman's arrival.

David kept quiet during dinner, only making the polite comments and responses required of a host. He sat at the far end of the long dining table, away from his aunt and Pastor Newman, between two gossipy matrons. They ignored his presence in their eagerness to share the latest rumors. David loathed being around such people, but tonight he desired anonymity and welcomed the screen from attention their noisy presence provided.

David hoped his aunt down at the other end of the table would keep Pastor Newman so occupied he wouldn't engage David in any revealing conversation in front of the others. David relaxed slightly as Pastor Newman, having read a recent dispatch from India, began an animated discussion with others around him of the exciting news about William Carey's translation of the New Testament into the Marathi language.

Everyone else enjoyed themselves, but David sat picking at his food. At last the meal drew to a close.

"Pastor Newman, would you care for some flummery?" Aunt Abigail asked. "An old family recipe my grand sires brought over from Lancashire."

"I remember your luscious pudding well!" Pastor Newman said. "But no, thank you. I can't eat another bite, presently. Later, perhaps." He patted his stomach. "You've stuffed me like a Christmas goose!" Aunt Abigail and others chuckled at his comment. Dr. Newman sighed and said, "I must speak a private word with young David in your husband's library, if I may."

David grew pale at this startling request. None of those around him seemed to notice, as the two female talebearers beside David picked up their scandalous blather where they'd left off.

"Make yourself at home," Aunt Abigail said to Dr. Newman. "You spent many hours in that library when you studied as a young pastor living near."

"Blessed days, back then," Pastor Newman said. "I've missed your late husband and his books."

David stood, excused himself and followed as Pastor Newman led the way into the paneled library and closed the walnut sliding doors behind him. Uncle Linus had been a book collector as well as a bookseller and merchant. Brown University Library received most of his personal literature collection upon his death, but a good sampling remained on the floor to ceiling shelves of the library.

Pastor Newman gestured toward two Queen Anne chairs beside the bay window. David sat down in the far chair, gripping the leather arms. Pastor Newman stirred up the coals in the Franklin stove and added fresh wood before sitting down in the other chair. "That's better," he said. He paused while a longcase clock sounded the hour. His kindly eyes studied David while he gathered his thoughts before speaking. Rather than castigation, the Pastor's wizened face bore an expression of heartfelt concern. David fought to keep from squirming under his gentle gaze. The clock finished chiming. The room became quiet save for beats of the brass pendulum, swinging at a pace slower than the pounding of David's heart.

"You have an outstanding heritage, David," Pastor Newman

began in measured tones. "Your grandfather and father were notable Baptist preachers, your late uncle a dedicated Christian layman. My blessed privilege to know them all and co-labor with them on occasion. Your grandfather was, as I remember, a great admirer of David Brainerd, the missionary to the Indians."

"They were classmates at Yale," said David. Hot and uncomfortable at the direction Pastor Newman took, beads of sweat formed on his brow.

"He named your father after him," Pastor Newman continued. "And you bear your father's name, as well--'David Brainerd Youngman.'" Pastor Newman began advancing the point. "Some of your school friends are asking about you."

"Who's that?" David asked. He drew out his handkerchief, wiping perspiration from his forehead. He knew the identity of the 'school friends,' but feigned ignorance shielded him, giving him something to say in response.

"Theophilus Wilson and Robert Thacker, among others. You attended one of their cowshed prayer meetings this past term."

"Merely an exercise in piety," David said, parrying the subject with a sanctimonious lie. "The earnestness of those involved impressed me." True in part but not the whole.

"You grew agitated and ran from that meeting," said Pastor Newman.

David swallowed. "I found the atmosphere uncomfortable and departed." True again. David said no more than necessary while enduring this inquiry.

"Tell me honestly, is God calling you to serve Him in a specific way?"

"I . . . . "David opened his mouth to give an excuse. He failed, fell silent and turned away.

'David, God has a purpose for your life." Pastor Newman's soft, tender tones cut David's heart like hardened steel blades. "Your parents prayed for this often in your early childhood. They prayed you'd continue in the ministry God had given them."

A sudden coldness hit David to the core. "I . . . I don't remember anything about that."

"Perhaps an answer to those prayers came in that student prayer meeting." Pastor Newman said. "Seems God is calling you to bring the good news of salvation to many souls in desperate need."

"Why do you think that?" David said. He refused to admit to Pastor Newman that he had hit the target.

"A deduction, a supposition on my part perhaps," said Pastor Newman. "Am I correct?"

David's hands tightened into fists. He forced himself to loosen them. Evading a direct confession, he muttered, "Maybe."

"Permit me to deduce, to suppose, further," said Pastor Newman. "Let's say God's leading you where you don't want to go. Your hatred of Indians is well known. Perhaps you're unwilling to yield that hatred to the Lord."

"Indians killed my parents!" David's voice rose. He blushed and pulled at his collar, embarrassed the truth about him appeared so evident.

"But it wasn't *all* Indians who killed them, just those few raiders from a particular village from a particular tribe," Pastor Newman continued. "But your malevolence runs broadly. Here it is, Christmas Eve, yet you know little of the spirit of forgiveness coming from the Christ of Christmas."

"How would you feel?" David countered.

Pastor Newman pressed his point. "How does *God* feel? On the first Christmas, 'God so loved the world' and sent His only begotten Son, knowing full well the very world of men He so loved would reject and slay His Son. Yet, because of those lost sinners, Jesus still came, suffered, died and rose again. Remember Christ's prayer from the cross, 'Father, forgive them for they know not what they do?' His forgiveness even includes mankind who crucified Him."

Heat flushed through David's body. "Merciless brutes killed my parents! I can't love them, and don't ask God to love them either."

"But God *is* love, David. He doesn't have to make Himself love—His nature is sacrificial love," Pastor Newman said. "Christ loves all men and died that all might receive forgiveness from sin, offering His mercy even to merciless killers. I venture to guess He's appointed you to bear the message of that forgiveness."

"And forget the shouts of my father?! The scream of my mother?!" David snapped. Intense pain inside boiled over. "I won't! I can't!"

"No one asks that of you, David, and God hasn't forgotten them either," Pastor Newman said. "They were slain in His service. The Psalmist wrote, 'Precious in the sight of the Lord is the death of His saints.' God knows and understands your hurt, your loss, and feels it with you. Others have felt such loss, and grace from Jesus Christ has helped them through it. He offers you that grace as well."

David jerked himself to his feet. "Sir, I really must be going."

Pastor Newman put his hand on David's arm, stopping him. "Bear with me. I have a story to tell you, one of the reasons for this talk. May I?"

David slumped back into his chair. "If you must, sir."

"Please bear with me, David," Pastor Newman said. He stood and gazed out the window, not seeing the wintry night, but viewing something in his mind's eye, a long ago scene. "Picture a young man, a bit older than yourself, preparing for the ministry. Hatred overshadows that young man's life too. For him, it's hatred of the French. They killed his two older brothers during the Ft. Ticonderoga Campaign back in 1760. The young man was only a little boy then, like you when your parents died. He adored his brothers, and from that time he nurtures a growing, bitter hatred for the

French.

Sixteen years later come Lexington, Concord and Bunker Hill. The pastor the young man now studies under is a ranking militia officer. The young man takes a lieutenant's commission, serving as his aide. The pastor joins General Washington's staff, bringing the young lieutenant with him. Seeking help against the British, Congress forms an alliance with the French. General Washington appoints that young man as an interpreter and liaison with French troops landing here in Rhode Island."

"But, as you say, he hates the French," David's tension subsided a little. The fascinating account drew him in.

"Oh, he does indeed hate the French!" Pastor Newman continued. "He's learned about them, studied their culture and history, became fluent in their language as well. All for *revenge* someday—for use in violent retribution against them. Now he must assist the abhorrent French in every way possible rather than avenge his brothers. Torn between hatred and patriotism, the young man decides to go away, though he'll become an outcast, no better than a Tory. He's in the very act of writing his resignation, quitting his commission, when his pastor discovers it."

"And the pastor stopped him?" David asked.

"All that pastor can do is counsel him," Pastor Newman answered, "much as I'm counseling you. He urges the young lieutenant to submit his will to the Savior, yield his hate, perform his duty. A great spiritual struggle within that young man's heart. Praying all night in his quarters. By the grace of God, he yields his heart. An enormous weight passes from him. God blesses. Good things happen in his life, in his service to his country and in ministry to others from that time."

"A different situation," David said. "The French helped us win at Yorktown."

"No way of the young man knowing that will come," Pastor Newman explained. "Many dark days lie ahead before the Lord guides to Yorktown. I'm not saying final victory is due alone to that young lieutenant's submission and service, but later years of fruitful pastoral ministry do grow from victory over his hate." The elderly pastor turned from the window and met David's gaze. "I should know. I was that young officer."

"You struggled with hate?" David said. Hard to imagine Dr. Newman as anything but one of the kindest, most compassionate men he'd ever known.

"I take no credit for the transformation in my life. It's all the Lord's doing. He convicted my heart, forgave my sin, and released me from my bondage in bitterness. He will transform you too, David, if you'll surrender your will to Him. He wants your parents' death to bring victory not defeat. He calls you as an the agent of that victory."

"Me?! How could that be possible?"

The pastor sat down and leaned toward David. "Those walking in the darkness of sin slew your parents. Now you might bring light, the gospel light, into that darkness."

"Bring the gospel to savage killers?!"

Pastor Newman leaned back in his chair. "Some in Christian circles condemn the revival in foreign missionary work we've seen in recent years. They're appalled that civilized men would 'take the holy gospel to the heathen.' But Scripture tells us 'God is not willing that any should perish.' Savage or civilized, all men are sinners in need of the Savior. Proclaiming the good news of salvation is every Christian's sacred commission."

"So you say."

"So our Lord Jesus Himself says, 'Go ye into *all* the world and preach to gospel to *every* creature,'" Pastor Newman said. "Who will warn those woodland people to escape the destruction of their souls if you disobey God's call? The tenth chapter of the Epistle to the Romans makes it clear, 'How will they believe in him of whom they have not heard, and how shall they hear without a preacher?' It's a simple truth: People must understand certain basic things about sin and about Jesus Christ to be saved. Someone must tell them."

David's stomach tightened. "Someone else, perhaps. Theo or Robert, not me!"

"If God has called *you*, David. *You* alone must fulfill that call," Pastor Newman said. "The eternal destiny of others depends on your obedience."

"What those Indians did to me and my parents can't be merely brushed aside!" Hot tears welled up in David's eyes. His temples throbbed.

Pastor Newman drew folded sheets of paper from his pocket. "Perhaps you're familiar with these words: '. . . For I am ready not to be bound only but to die for the name of the Lord Jesus.' Do you know who wrote those words?"

"The Apostle Paul, I suppose." David wiped his palms again along his trousers, unsure where this quotation now led the conversation.

"Paul's words, yes, but paraphrased by your father as he closed this long letter written to me the Christmas just before he died," Pastor Newman said, showing the handwritten pages.

"My father's words written to you?"

"Yes. We began collaboration on a translation of the New Testament he hoped to make for those tribes he evangelized. Regular correspondence between us as I advised him." Pastor Newman handed David the sheets of paper. "Take the letter. Keep it. Read it for yourself. Re-read it many times. Let your father speak to you."

David's hands trembled as he stared down at the ink on the paper. "My father wrote this?"

"Yes, and from what I read there, it's almost as if he wrote it to you now as much as he to me back then. You'll see he was well aware of dangers he faced and risks taken, knew of immanent trouble. You'll also read there he knew no greater cause than the glorious gospel of his Savior, Jesus Christ. It's to this same great cause God is calling you."

"I'm not so sure." David glanced away.

"You trusted Christ for your own salvation, David. Seven years old, I believe. Your father mentions it in his letter. Please read it to me."

David unfolded the pages and began to read aloud:

My Dear Newman,

I write to you of some joyful news!

The work here has been a hard one. Progress in the Gospel is slow. Reaching out to these tribes who have no concept of our God or of His Word can only progress with the patience our Lord supplies. I must teach them before I may reach them. I take for my model the way the Apostle Paul reached out to those at Lystra and at Mar's Hill, who also knew nothing of the True God, beginning with the basics of Creation and moving on from there.

Language study has advanced greatly since we accepted the tribal chief's invitation to establish this mission station closer to the native villages. Now we have daily interaction with the people and learn much from them. Young Davy surpasses us all. Playing with the Indian children has given him a practical knowledge of their tongue. He learns new words all the time and teaches them to his mother and me.

While learning their language, I preached my way through the four gospels. Enclosed with this letter is a copy of notes I made while doing that. They will assist us in our translation work.

Recently I felt confident enough to begin preaching directly in their tongue, without an interpreter, continuing through the Book of Acts.

Moving away from safety of the White settlements and preaching these new messages on my own has demonstrated our genuine love for these people. A greater interest stirs among them. Larger groups come to listen. Instead of ten or fifteen, I speak to twenty or thirty, sometimes more. Little spiritual response has come from this as of yet, but God is always good. At a time when I'd let discouragement about so little to show for our efforts creep upon me, the Lord encouraged my heart greatly in the work of His Gospel, showing me unexpected fruit . . ."

David paused. His thoughts drawn back to that time, years before, living with his parents on the mission station inside Indian territory . . .

He saw again his mother saying to his father, "Your preaching improves each time, Dear. You hardly faltered today. I could follow almost everything you said."

"But not much fruit so far, for all the effort," Missionary Youngman said.

"But they continue coming to hear you just the same," insisted his wife.

"Oh, Betsy, sometimes I wonder if I'm getting through at all or just providing some odd form of entertainment for them," he said.

David's mother consoled, "You got through to one today, Dear, a little boy."

"Really?" he asked. "Is it *Abook-sigun* or *Mak-kapitew*? Did he stay for me to talk with him?"

"It's someone else, and he does want to tell you about it," she said.

"Who?" he asked.

"Our son, Davy!"

"Davy?!"

"God has worked in his heart!" she said, and called, "Davy, Papa will talk with you now."

Young Davy came running over, excited and earnest. "Papa! Papa! I did what you said!"

"Did what?" asked the father.

"I prayed to God, as you told us," said the son. "I believed

49

on the Lord Jesus just like that man in your sermon today!"

"The Philippian Jailer?" said Davy's father. "I had trouble explaining him in their language."

Young Davy said, "But I heard you. I understood. You said Paul told him, 'Believe on the Lord Jesus Christ, and you will be saved' and that's what I did."

"Asking God to save you from sin and trusting Jesus to be your savior?" asked his father.

"Yes! Like how you told the people. I prayed and I asked."

His father picked him up and swung him around with joy. "Oh, Davy! God be praised! This is wonderful news! Let us pray and give thanks!"

The three Youngmans knelt together in front of the brush arbor. David's father put his hand on one of the lad's shoulders, and Mrs. Youngman placed her hand on top of the other.

"Dear Lord, thank you for Davy's salvation. Use him someday in Thy service that other's might also hear and believe. . ."

* * * * *

David lowered the pages of the letter, too choked up to continue reading. Hot tears ran down his cheeks. The old wound raw again.

Pastor Newman said, "How your parents rejoiced!"

"They did. I'd . . . I'd forgotten." David admitted.

"You may have forgotten, and you may try to run away now, but because of your salvation, the Holy Spirit is always within you," Pastor Newman said. "Wherever you run, He'll always be there chastening, convicting, calling you back to Himself."

David wiped away angry tears with his sleeves, attempting to hide the issue. "Who said anything about running away?"

"The marks of it are on you," Pastor Newman said. "Your thoughts, your actions, read like an open book because I've been in your shoes. I know three choices you're considering: Obeying this call of God; resisting it in bitterness; or fleeing from it. You're a young man of action. If you won't obey, you'll flee rather than decline in personal stagnation."

David stiffened and spoke through clenched teeth. "It's impossible for me to forgive those killers for what they did to me and my parents!"

"Through Jesus Christ *all* forgiveness is possible," Pastor Newman countered. "Twice now you've said "what they did to *ME* and my parents," putting the "me" first and then your parents."

David shrugged it off. "A slip of grammar."

"Others have suffered as well," said Pastor Newman. "The people your parents were reaching have faced hard times. Disease and strife with encroaching settlers have taken a toll on them. They've been pushed farther west. British interests from Canada have stirred up warfare among the tribes against American Whites and against each other. Those people need you. This could mean a spiritual healing for both you and for them."

"I wouldn't know how to go about it."

"What God commands His servants to do, He gives them power to fulfill by His Spirit. He sends others to help along the way. Let me mentor you in the ministry while you finish at the University. I will help you gather support from the Baptist associations. Above all, go out to those people!"

David pushed himself back into the chair. "I'd rather go away than go to *them!*" He bit off each word. Truth trapped him by its convicting power.

Pastor Newman maintained his calm. "There. You've honestly said it! Go away, and you'll miss the great joy the Lord desires for you in fulfilling His purpose for your life. Your parents knew that joy, desired for you to know it too."

David's head ached. He rubbed his pounding temples. "Sir, are you about finished?"

"I wouldn't do right as your pastor without leaving a sober warning."

"What kind of warning?" David asked, fearing what this might be.

"There's a Bible on the bookstand beside you," Pastor Newman said, nodding toward the stand. "Please read to me from the Old Testament Book of Jonah."

"Why Jonah?"

"Consider the first chapter, verse seventeen," Pastor Newman said.

David reached for the large Bible and rested it upon his lap. He turned pages to the passage and read, "'Now the LORD had prepared a great fish to swallow up Jonah. And Jonah was in the belly of the fish three days and three nights.'"

"You see there Jonah's disobedience didn't catch the Lord unaware," Pastor Newman explained. "He foresaw the prophet's actions and prepared for them. I suggest you read all of that account. Contemplate your own choices. Like Jonah, if you flee God's will, you may be running away into trouble. You'll endanger others wherever you go. Who knows what the cost may be if your Heavenly Father must reach out in love and chasten you back to Himself?"

David closed the Bible, saying. "I doubt God concerns Himself with one as unimportant as me."

"Oh, but your Heavenly Father does concern Himself intimately with His chosen messenger, with His message and with the men He desires to receive it—that's what you'll find in the Book of Jonah. I will pray for safety, for you and those around you." He stood and rested his hand upon David's shoulder. "My door will always be open for you, David, when you're ready to accept God's call."

Pastor Newman slid the doors open and walked from the

library.

David remained slumped in his chair, exhausted by the ordeal and stunned by the revelation of so much he had thought hidden about himself. He rubbed his palms along the leather arms of the chair. He glanced down at the letter from his father, shaken by Pastor Newman's counsel, and struggled with fires of conviction raging in his heart. He knew the truth of what Pastor Newman said, but he could not yield himself to it. This letter from his father made it worse. With David's angry rebellion toward God out in the open now, he resented his father for allowing all the bad to happen. The cheerful voice of his aunt broke his troubled thoughts.

"Davy, come by the fire and join with us in some carols." she said from the open door. She returned back to the parlor.

David folded the letter and opened the Bible. He flipped through the book at random, seeking a place to deposit the letter and be rid of it. The pages came open again the first chapter of Jonah. The facing page bore an illustration. A woodcut depicted an ancient sailing vessel caught in a raging tempest. An immense whale trailed in the ship's wake. David's incensed imagination pictured that scene coming alive—*waves crashing against the ship's hull, swamping its deck; wind howling, breaking its mast; the desperate crew casting the Disobedient Prophet overboard; and the whale's enormous mouth gaping open above the foamy surface and receiving him.* David shook himself from the dark daydream. He thrust the letter into the Bible and snapped its pages closed.

David skulked back from the library. People in the parlor sang a carol proclaiming the joy of Christmas, but David's troubled heart distanced itself from joy. He paused, adjusted his clothing, slipped into the parlor and took a lone chair at the opposite end. Aunt Abigail, Pastor Newman, and the other guests enjoyed themselves around the hearth, roasting chestnuts and popping corn. They sang several other carols and read the nativity story from the Gospels of Matthew and Luke.

David hunched in his cold corner, removed from the fire and festivity. He kept his face impassive but brooded in his thoughts. Everything about Christmas disturbed him that night, reminding him of his call to preach the gospel. He fidgeted through the proceedings.

A desperate, nervous energy built inside him. An urge arose to get away from Christmas and all it entailed.

The other guests settled back as Pastor Newman (coaxed by Aunt Abigail) shared a stirring first-hand account of crossing the Delaware with Washington's desperate army on that snowy Christmas night in 1776. Everyone gave the pastor's story rapt attention. As the pastor described the climatic surprise and defeat of the Hessians the next morning at Trenton, David kissed Aunt Abigail's forehead and excused himself for the night.

David stole off to his room but didn't go to bed. He dashed off a brief note to his aunt, a lie about visiting Marcus for the rest of his break. He stuffed essential clothing into his saddle bags. He gathered the portion of the inheritance granted so far by his uncle's will into his money bag. Out of habit, He reached for his Bible, paused and set it back on the nightstand.

David placed the note on the kitchen counter. He put on his winter coat, hat, gloves and boots. He slipped out the back as the parlor gathering sang, "O Come, O Come, Emmanuel."

David's horse balked at leaving the comforts of the stall, but David saddled him and forced him out into the night air. He walked the animal around the house. Lights blazed gaily from the parlor windows out upon the snowy yard. No one noticed as he passed. The muffled voices within sang from "God Rest Ye Merry, Gentlemen:"

"Now to the Lord sing praises.

All you within this place,

And with true love and brotherhood

Each other now embrace . . ."

David led the horse down to the road and mounted. He rode out of the town, a lone figure heading down a dark, road. The wintry night grew colder as he rode the nine miles to Newport. His heart grew colder still.

PART THREE: THE FLIGHT

Jonah 1:3c *". . . and he found a ship going to Tarshish:*

so he paid the fare thereof . . ."

CHAPTER SEVEN

"I can't say 'farewell,' only 'come back!'"

A FARM OUTSIDE NEWPORT

CHRISTMAS MORNING 1811

By previous arrangement, David woke Marcus by rapping on his bedroom window. Marcus opened the window, yawning and rubbing his sleepy eyes.

"You ready to leave?" David whispered.

"You really are serious about this, aren't you?" Marcus whispered back.

"I'm going whether you come along or not," David said.

"What about all my tools?"

"Leave them," David said. "They'll slow us down. We'll buy what you need when we get to Paris."

"Give me a few minutes to gather clothes, then."

"Hurry!" David said, looking around at the first gray light of the approaching dawn. "I thought you'd be all ready! Hasseltine's sailing at sunrise. I must be aboard."

"Meet you in front," Marcus said, and closed the window.

David came around the house to the front porch. He slipped back a step when he saw what awaited him there. Nancy stood out on the cold porch in her robe, night cap and carpet slippers, arms folded across her chest. Putting God out of his mind had put Nancy out too, and he hadn't prepared for this situation. He'd hoped she'd remain asleep when he called for Marcus. Her stern expression warned him of her displeasure.

"I brought you this horse as a Christmas present," David said, avoiding her eyes, busying himself with tying the animal's reins to a post. His selfish plans had so consumed his attention he hadn't considered giving her any kind of gift. His quick lie seemed a way to mask that and possibly defuse her unhappiness with him. The horse had to be left behind anyway.

"I don't want your horse," she said, "or anything else aiding in your plans."

"What plans?" he asked.

"You didn't come bringing a gift," she said. "You're running away."

David shot a glance at her, at a loss for words to explain it to her. He pulled his saddle bags off the animal and glanced out toward the road.

Nancy stepped from the porch. "Don't run, Davy! I know it's out of place for a young female to speak this way, but there's no time. I must be blunt: I'd hoped for much more between us, but not now."

"Maybe there could be someday," David said.

"Not if you're running off to France."

Her knowledge of his intentions caught him off guard. Doubt gnawed at his resolution. He steeled himself against it and against her influence, turned to her and said, "Perhaps I'll send for you in time."

"I won't come," she said. "Not in time. *Not ever!*"

"I'll go on writing you," he said, trying to find some way to turn her back to himself, to leave a door open.

She slammed that door shut. "I won't read your letters anymore."

"But I thought you've begun to care for me."

"I do care," she said, voice choking, "very much." Her eyes welled up with tears. "That's why I won't come to you or even read your letters. The Bible asks, 'Can two walk together unless they be agreed?' I've dedicated my life to serve the Lord Jesus Christ. I've been praying for a husband with the same dedication. After we'd talked in Providence, after I read your wonderful letters—about your heart opening to God—I felt you might be the one for whom I've prayed. If there's a future for us some day, it will be walking together *in* the service of the Lord, not running *from* Him."

David had never imagined Nancy this way—fighting back her tears, strong and unflinching in heartfelt conviction. Her steadfastness unnerved him.

They stood a moment, the fog of their breath hanging in the air. Nancy's sad eyes touched his soul. He could not meet her gaze. Marcus broke the stand-off, sneaking out on the porch lugging an old portmanteau. Seeing Nancy there outside startled him, and he dropped the luggage with a thud.

"Marcus, what on earth did you tell her?' David snapped.

Marcus glanced sheepishly at his sister and shrugged. "Sorry, Davy. Hearing you'd been to town without coming to see her upset her. She wheedled it out of me about going to the harborside tavern. I barely told her anything more. The next day, Robert Thacker, one of your college friends, came by picking up a hat for his fiancee. Nancy asked him about you. From there she came to conclusions all on her own."

David brushed the snow from his saddle bags and turned to leave. Nancy stepped into his path, blocking his way and forcing him to look her in the eye. Chin up, her face flushed and determined, she said, "David Youngman, if it's God's will for us to be together, I'll go anywhere with you in that will. To the Indians, the West Indies or far away India—but I'm going to draw near to God, not run from Him. I'll be waiting here, praying for you to turn back to Him again."

David glanced away, crushed and cold inside. He sighed and stepped around her. "Then it's 'good-bye,' Nan," he said in a low voice.

"I can't say 'farewell,' only 'come back!'" she whispered as he passed.

David slung the saddle bags over his shoulder, set his grim face toward Newport, trudging away in the snow.

Marcus picked up his baggage. "Good-bye, Nan."

Nancy wiped her eyes and hugged her brother. "I'm angry with you, Marcus, for being part of this, but Davy needs someone to watch out for him. You take care and take care of Davy for me, please!"

"I'll try," Marcus said, he kissed her tear-dampened cheek and trotted off after David.

Nancy sank to her knees in the snow, praying, shoulders shaking with her sobs.

Jonah 1:5c *". . . but Jonah was gone down into the sides of the ship; and he lay, and was fast asleep."*

CHAPTER EIGHT

"Merry Christmas, indeed!"

ABOARD THE MERCHANT BRIG POCASSETT

LONG ISLAND SOUND

CHRISTMAS DAY 1811

The two young men hurried through the sleeping town and down to the harbor. The docks lay quiet in the frosty air. Only one ship bustled with activity. The edge of dawn showed crimson beyond the island. Men on board cleared accumulated snow from the ship's deck and tackle. A stout man in a dark blue pea coat stood at the top of the gangplank, puffing on his pipe and making notations in a ledger.

"Merry Christmas, Captain Hasseltine!" David called.

"Merry Christmas!" echoed Marcus.

The captain smiled and pointed his pipe stem at them "Merry Christmas, my lads! Come to see me off or come to sail with me?"

"To sail with you today!" David said.

"In spite of the blockade," said Marcus.

Hasseltine laughed. "Well, that's the spirit if you want to get ahead in this world! Come aboard, come aboard, my lads. I've hoped you'd come. Welcome aboard the good ship *Pocassett*. Get you up on the quarterdeck there. Ask for Mr. Lattimore, he's second officer and acting ship's clerk. He'll sign you in on the log, collect your fare, and have one of the cabin boys show you accommodations, such as we have."

The rising sun gleamed above the eastern hills. The hands dropped moorings, weighed anchor and hoisted sails. In honor of the day, they sang a rousing Christmas carol as they worked.

The *Pocassett* glided from the quay, left the harbor and headed out into Narragansett Bay. The ship turned south, put on more sail and picked up speed. The snowy Rhode Island shoreline disappeared behind them.

The cries of the gulls, the ship plunging through the waves, and the brisk ocean breeze all numbed the cares of David's embattled heart. *At last, heading away.*

Everything seemed peaceful and calm and going according to his plan.

Fatigue swept over him. David shuddered and kept his balance by gripping the rail. He took leave of those on deck and headed below. Weary from inner struggles and traveling through the night, he flopped onto his berth fully clothed and fell into a deep sleep. David slept through the morning and into the early afternoon.

Ever mindful of the prowling British, the blockade runners kept careful watch around the compass points. A hand loft in the foretop called down a warning. Mr. Lattimore relayed it to Captain Hasseltine beside the helm, "Foretop reports something off the port bow, sir."

The captain's eyes strained into the distance, seeking anything out of place. *Something there?* He lifted his telescope and scanned the north horizon again. *Something is there!* He fixed his scope on a dark shape emerging from the mouth of the Sakonmet River. Without hesitation, he bellowed, "All hands on deck! Hard to starboard!."

"All hands on deck!" cried Mr. Lattimore.

"Hard to starboard!" repeated the helmsman.

"Change course, sou' by sou'east" Hasseltine commanded.

"Course heading sou' by sou'east," said the helmsman as he turned the ship's wheel.

Hasseltine pointed off to the right. "To those clouds building there!"

"Aye, sir," acknowledged the helmsman.

Marcus had been enjoying the voyage, but now the ship's crew scurried aloft and vessel turned, heading toward angry looking clouds. He approached Hasseltine. "Captain, is something wrong?"

Hasseltine kept the telescope to his eye as the ship came about and said, "Sail behind us to starboard and closing fast."

Marcus turned, strained with his own eyes and saw the dark shape far behind them. "Another merchant ship? Fishermen? A whaler perhaps?"

"Not the way she's bearing down on us. Bet my life it's that British frigate!" said Hasseltine. "Had their spies back in Newport, no doubt!" He called down to the crewmen assembled on the main deck, "Hands aloft! All sails, ta'gallants and stun'sils! Shake out every inch of canvas!" He grinned at Marcus. "We'll give 'em a merry chase!"

"Can they catch you?"

"Ha! The *Pocassett's* swifter than that British tub!" Hasseltine boasted. "And I know a trick or two. Storm coming up from the southeast. We'll lose him running towards it. Into it, if need be. Few ships tack into the wind better than this one."

The wind sang through the taught ropes as the *Pocassett* raced ahead. The dark sails behind diminished a bit in size.

Hasseltine rubs his hand together, confident of his ship and his crew. "That's showing 'em!"

As ever before, *Pocassett* fled the pursuing danger smoothly, effortlessly—

The *Pocassett* shuddered under a thunderous jolt! Timbers cracked and split. Ropes snapped.

Hands cried out, "Look out! Take cover!"

The mainmast toppled over with a tremendous crash, ripping the top and top-gallant sections off the foremast cascading down with it. A jumbled heap of spars, tangled ropes and torn sail cloth littered the main deck of what had been a trim vessel moments before.

Like a giant fallen tree, the mainmast hung at a sharp angle over the port side, sails and all. Top mast and top-gallant mast sections dragged in the water pulling the ship down in a list to port. The wreckage acted like a sea anchor, bringing the *Pocassett* to a halt and swinging her broadside toward on-coming frigate.

"What's happened?!" Marcus cried.

Hasseltine struck his leg in frustration. "Merry Christmas, indeed! We've lost our main mast, and it's fouled other rigging! Never seen the like before. Like the hand of God reached down and snapped it like a twig!"

He surveyed the British frigate bearing down on him. Deflated in spirit, he snapped his telescope closed and hung his head. "They'll have us now."

Down below, David slept on, dead to the world. The jolt, crash and noises up above on deck and the list of the ship couldn't rouse him.

Swift and inexorable, the British man o' war tacked in. A momentary puff of smoke dispersed in the breeze following the dull boom of a long 9-pounder. A cannon ball whizzed past the wounded *Pocassett's* bow and splashed into blue-gray waves beyond.

"As if he needs us to heave to," Hasseltine grumbled. "We're already dead in the water. Now he'll have his way with us."

The frigate hove-to a short distance away. Her white battle ensign rippled in the stiff breeze. Red gun ports facing the *Poccassett* bristled with the black muzzles of eighteen 24-pounder carronades. Two 42-pounder carronades threatened from the frigate's quarterdeck. Red-coated marines, muskets ready, lined her rails and stood aloft in her rigging. One pointed a swivel-gun down from her fighting-top. Blue-coated officers scanned the wrecked and helpless ship with their spyglasses. An angry voice bellowed across, "Ahoy! Stand-by to be boarded!"

Two longboats launched from the frigate. They pulled across the tossing waves and came past the wreckage alongside. A dozen marines, bayonets ready, swarmed onto the sloping deck and formed a defensive semi-circle by the gangway. A score of sailors followed, armed with pistols and naked cutlasses. A moment later two dour men in blue uniform, swords in hand, climbed aboard. The two officers paused a moment, looking the *Pocassett* over, assessing her damage with a professional eye.

The grim-faced, older of the two approached Captain Hasseltine. "I'm Captain Richard Forester of His Britannic Majesty's frigate, *Leviathan*." He nodded toward the tall, dour officer beside him. "My first officer, Lieutenant Sturndale."

Hasseltine touched the brim of his hat in response. "Captain Edward Hasseltine of the merchantman *Pocassett*. What business is this stopping an American ship in American waters?!"

Captain Forester, grim and businesslike, ignored Hasseltine's question. "Mr. Sturndale, turn all their hands out. Check their log," he said. "I want every man giving an English town as his origin."

The dour officer said, "Aye, sir!"

The British seamen herded Hasseltine's crewmen together out on the deck at gunpoint. The marines kept them under a watchful eye. Down below, rough hands tumbled sleeping David out of his berth.

"What . . . what goes on here!" he shouted. He struggled, both in coming to his feet on the angled deck and in recognizing his unfamiliar surroundings. He remembered being on the *Pocassett*. He thought Hasseltine's crewmen dragged him out. "That's a rude way to treat your passengers! I shall protest to your captain."

"I'll show you rude!" said one of the men. The back of his

hand struck David across the side of his face, splitting his lip, knocking him down. When David pulled himself up again, he noticed the cutlasses in the men's hands and the pistols in their belts.

"Come along, you!" One of them barked, jerking his head toward the door and swatting David with the flat of his cutlass. David staggered up on deck and joined Marcus and Hasseltine's crew cowering there.

The lieutenant reported to Captain Forester, put hand to his hat in salute and handed him a sheet of paper. He pointed out notations he'd made. "Copied 'em from the ship's log, sir. These are the names and places."

Forester read down the list. "Ha-hmm! Thirteen men appear to be British subjects. We'll take them into the service of their king. Very good, Mr. Sturndale." He handed the list back to the lieutenant.

"Thank you, sir." said Sturndale.

"I must protest, captain!" shouted Hasseltine. "That's more than half my men!"

"I'll waste no time with your feeble protests!" Captain Forester snapped. "The Royal Navy struggles with the Corsican Tyrant, and I'll take every able bodied Englishman for my crew."

"Not me!" Marcus cried.

"Captain Hasseltine, what about us?" David asked.

"Those two young men are paid passengers!" Hasseltine said.

"Their names?" asked Captain Forester.

"David Youngman," said David.

"Marcus Trent," added Marcus.

Sturndale looked down the page. "The log lists 'Portsmouth' as origin for both."

"Portsmouth, England, we'll assume," said Captain Forester.

"No! Portsmouth in Rhode Island!" David protested.

"We're Americans!" shouted Marcus.

"Silence!" snapped Sturndale. He turned back to his captain. "Sir! Shall I bring over a prize crew?"

"No. There'll be no sailing this one to Halifax today," said Captain Forester. "Too much damage with this storm coming on. Set prisoners to work. Jettison enough debris to right this ship and clear the cargo hatches. Leave the rest. Heave their rice overboard, then transfer the new men to *Leviathan*."

"Aye, aye, sir!" Sturndale said, saluting his captain.

"Overboard?!" shrieked Hasseltine. "This is an outrage!"

Forester turned on the merchant, his composure even grimmer. "Hasseltine, you're the outrage! You flaunted our blockade again and again! But not this time. Be thankful I don't send your vessel to the bottom of the sea. By the looks of this wreckage, Divine Providence has done the work for us this day. We'll leave you to His mercy and the storm."

Hasseltine collapsed against a bulkhead, wailing, "Of all the foul luck! I'm ruined! Ruined!"

Jonah 1:17a *"Now the LORD had prepared*

a great fish to swallow up Jonah . . ."

CHAPTER NINE

"Why have you plagued my ship?"

ON BOARD H.M.S. LEVIATAN

OFF THE NEW ENGLAND COAST

CHRISTMAS WEEK 1811

David, Marcus and the miserable men of the *Pocasset* kept under guard hacked at the ropes entangling the wrecked masts, sails and rigging and freed the brig from the debris. Once the ship righted itself, the prisoners hauled heavy grain sacks up from the hold and heaved them over the side.

They finished their involuntary labor with the storm almost upon them. Thunder rumbled overhead as they rowed across the rising swells and white caps to the British vessel. The men were forced into bailing the overloaded longboats lest the rough waters swamp them.

The British marines and sailors prodded their captives up the slippery ladder and onto the frigate's deck. Lieutenant Sturndale made the new men line up before the main mast while Captain Forester inspected the unfortunates.

One prisoner bolted for the rail, but seamen grabbed him before he leaped over the side. He struggled in their grasp until the marine sergeant clubbed him with a musket butt. The seamen dragged the dazed man back into the line.

Captain Forested bore his grim expression through the proceeding and said, "Mr. Sturndale, read them the Articles of War and enter them into the ship's log."

"Aye, aye, sir" said Sturndale.

"Then put 'em to work battening down for the storm," said Forester. "Let's see who are sailors among them."

He returned to the quarterdeck and observed the men, his hands clasped behind his rigid back.

Sturndale read the Royal Navy Articles of War aloud in a droning voice, which seemed to be a requirement of the articles themselves. David and Marcus were shocked on hearing the numerous infractions bringing an offender severe flogging or even death. Immediately after the reading, the officers compelled the new men in deck labor preparing for the storm. The bosun's mate applied a cane of rattan to the backsides of those failing to move quickly or perform to his expectations. He wrath fell roughest on David, because of his youth, and on Marcus, who lacked the skills and understanding of a sailor.

As soon as they could, David and Marcus tried reasoning with the first officer.

"Sir, there's been a terrible mistake,' David said. "I'm no sailor. I'm a student."

"I'm only a cobbler," said Marcus.

"'A student?' 'Only a cobbler?'" Sturndale mocked. "Grist for His Majesty's manpower mill, that's what you are. Enough with you! Back to work!"

A rude beginning to a harsh existence. The work proved hard and dangerous under the merciless discipline, nothing like their carefree boyhood experience aboard Uncle Linus' trading vessel. David and Marcus lashed down equipment on deck. They climbed the cold, slippery rigging and reefed the sails. Hesitation brought curses from the bosun and sharp strokes from his rattan.

Little consolation awaited them below decks. The men slept in tiers of swinging hammocks stacked four high and barely eighteen inches apart. The odors of cooking, the ship's heads and men's unwashed bodies fouled the air. Long at sea, much of the ship's perishable food had been consumed, the rest nearly rancid. Drinking water had grown stale and bitter from being kept so long in wooden casks.

After spending the rest of the cold, rainy Christmas afternoon in arduous toil on a pitching deck, David and Marcus sat down to a cheerless evening meal.

"H'enjoying yer Christmas dinner, lads?" mocked a scar-faced sailor.

"Aww! We's fresh out of roast goose an' plum puddin'," mocked his tattooed friend.

"But 'ere's peas' porridge an' salt pork to make up forrit!" joked the first sailor.

Both sailors laughed at their own jests. The plight of these two peculiar raw "impressments" provided riotous fun.

David held up a thick, round disk. The object dark and hard. "What's this supposed to be?"

"It's ship's biscuit, mate," said the pock-marked one.

"Biscuit?" Marcus said. "More like a rock."

"H'ain't no Christmas tea cake!" laughed the scar-faced sailor.

"Why are you all tapping them on the table that way?" Marcus asked.

"Brings out the weevils a'fore eatin'," pock-marked said.

"Don't go gnawin' at it dry," the scar-faced one cautioned. "Yew soak whut's left in yer grub."

"Otherwise yew'll break off all yer teeth like ol' George 'ere," the pock-marked sailor said.

"Not all, 'Arry!" corrected George, the scar-faced one. His

empty mouth struck a hideous grin. "Two or three still there!"

"Whut?! Thought I knocked the rest out last time we was in port!" said Harry, the pockmarked one.

"Davy, what's happened to us?" Marcus whispered.

"I'm afraid to think of it," David whispered back.

"My old boring life wasn't so bad after all. What I wouldn't give to be back at my cobbler's bench right now!"

"None o' that whisperin', blokes!" George scolded.

"Speak out, so we-ins can all hear it," said Harry.

"An' laugh at it!"

The storm increased in fury and tossed the vessel about, adding to hardship and discomfort. Waves battered the hull, came over the bow and bulwarks, swamped the weather decks. Life lines kept deck hands from being swept overboard. Even with hatches battened down, the frigate took on water through leaks in deck caulking and seams along the hull as powerful forces of ocean and atmosphere strained and stressed them. Water built up in the hold at an alarming rate. Teams manned the pumps around the clock keeping the flood in check.

Below decks, all hands led a brutal life. The pitch and roll of the ship made moving around difficult. Everything grew damp from exposure to the sheets of rain outside and the dripping of water from the decks above. Sleep in the swaying hammocks came only in fits and starts and brought little bodily rest.

The mood of officers and men turned fouler. Tempers flared. Harsher discipline fell on all. Aware of dangerous tensions rising between crew members, the captain gave strict warnings that fighting among the ranks would incur severe punishment. The officers pushed the men at various tasks, keeping them occupied and out of trouble.

The storm continued unabated the following day. The wind

shifted, multiplying misery as the tempest intensified into a dreaded nor'easter, keeping the ship from reaching open ocean. Bottled within the confines of Long Island Sound, the ship's crew struggled against the gale to keep the vessel from being driven onto shoals or against a rocky coast.

Accidents occurred, always with David present. These incidents increased in severity. When David took a turn at the pumps, the chain on the one he worked at broke. With one less pump, water in the hold rose at an alarming rate until difficult repairs brought the vital equipment into operation again.

The bosun compelled David to work on a gang securing stores in the dim light of the hold. Struck by a huge rogue wave, the ship lurched. A heavy barrel broke free, crashing against a stanchion. The cask's staves gave way, wasting precious gallons of remaining drinking water. The accident injured three men, but David escaped harm.

Later, David labored on his hands and knees scouring the galley deck. A rat, flushed from hiding by David's work, tipped over a cruse of oil. The spilled oil dripped onto a candle and ignited, causing a small fire. An uncontained fire posed great danger on a wooden ship. Two men joined David in the frantic effort smothering the flames. The fire burn the men on their faces, arms and hands, but David went unscathed.

When David worked on the gun deck with men refastening a hatch batten, chains securing a gun carriage nearby snapped. Carriage wheels squealing like a dozen pigs, the heavy carronade rumbled free across the pitching deck, crashing from bulkhead to bulkhead and gun to gun. David and four others chased the cannon down while trying to keep from being crushed by it. They succeeded in blocking its wheels and stopping the menace before it battered a hole through the hull. The incident left four men injured and dismounted two other carronades, but David came through unharmed again.

The crew's restlessness intensified with the mounting injuries. Bellow decks they grumbled, eyeing David with suspicion. Sensing a connection somehow with all the accidents, they badgered Marcus during his mess break about David being a link in the chain of mishaps.

"Ey, mate, whut's wit yer chum?" demanded George.

"What do you mean?" asked Marcus.

"'He's a rum bloke, tha' one. Ever'where he's workin', bad things seems ta happen," said Harry.

"Nonsense," Marcus defended. "I've known him for years."

"'E's pure bad luck, if yew ask me," George said.

"Aye! Regular 'Jonah,' he is!" Harry said.

"Steer clear of 'im or yew'll be next, mates!" George cautioned the others.

Night fell with all hands on edge. Tensions rose as the ocean storm came on even stronger.

Up on the quarterdeck, officers' shouted commands were barely audible in the howling wind. Captain Forester brought Lieutenant Sturndale into the shelter of his cabin to relay his orders.

"What a night!" Forester said, pulling off his rain gear. "Unusual, even for winter."

"Captain, I've never seen such a storm!" Sturndale said.

"Encountered two hurricanes on West Indies Station, when I was a midshipman and lieutenant," shouted Forester, "but weren't anything like this, caught in a narrow sound with no friendly port within easy sail."

Sturndale shouted, "It's as if God hounds this ship."

"If I were a theologian, I'd agree with you," shouted Forester. "Mr. Turner reports the main skys'ils have come unlashed again. This wind will shred 'em. Send hands aloft to secure main skys'ils."

"Aye, aye, sir!" Sturndale replied. He went out to the petty officer of the watch. Although the two men stood side by side, he cupped hands around his mouth and shouted, "Hands aloft! Secure main skys'ils!"

The petty officer relayed the order below to the duty crew, sheltered on the upper gun deck.

"'Secure main skys'ils?'" Marcus said, tying the straps of an oilskin rain hat under his chin. "What's that supposed to mean?"

David tying his hat's straps as well. "It means we have to climb up and tie them down."

Marcus groaned. "And it means being out in the storm."

"Even worse," David said. "They're the second tier of sails from the top."

Marcus groaned louder. "Oh, no!"

"Get going!" David said. "That beastly bosun comes with his rattan!"

The duty crew hurried up onto the cold, storm-lashed main deck.

Marcus shivered and peered upward at the top of the mast, veiled in rain and gloom above. "Up there in this wind and rain?!" he shouted, but no one heard him above the gale.

Lightning flashed as David, Marcus and others struggled up the rigging. They slipped on the wet ropes and swayed in the gusty wind.

Almost at the top, Marcus had trouble hanging on. "Davy, I'm slipping!"

David didn't hear him, but lighting flashed, revealing Marcus' struggle. David shouted, "Hang on, I'm coming!"

"Davy!" Marcus cried, fingers slipping away as David reached out to him.

David screamed, "Marcus!"

But his friend fell from view, tumbling toward the deck in the darkness below. David struggled against the wind, securing the top gallant sails on his mast, heart pounding from the effort and from fears for Marcus. He slipped, slid and swayed, descending back to the deck. Marcus had been carried to the wardroom set up as a sick bay. David went below to see Marcus, but the surgeon's assistant shoved him away and blocked the door.

Grief stricken, David returned to his hammock. He sorrowed for Marcus, lying now close to death, from what he heard. He sorrowed for himself, unaware of the sailors crouched in a dark corner, rolling dice.

"Roll again, mate," George said. "The dice'll tell us."

"As if we need 'em," said Harry.

"Shut up an' roll," rumbled George.

Harry rolled the dice. "The young bloke in the hammock. 'Tis him for sure."

"Figgered so," George sneered. "The *student!*"

"Can't just slit his throat. Make it look like a fight," Harry said.

"H'eas'ly done!" George leered. The rough sailor pulled out his knife. A quick slash cut the rope at one end of David's hammock.

David tumbled onto the deck. He raised his head, rubbing his bruised skull. "Hey! What is this?!"

"Pipe down!" Yelled a nearby sleeper, roused by the commotion.

George held his knife low, menacing, like his voice. "All right, mate. This 'ere ship 'as been dogged by bad luck since we took on yer lot."

"We rolled the dice an' 'tis yew they picked," said Harry.

George jabbed his knife at David. "Yew whut brung bad luck

on us."

David dodged the jab and backed away. He slipped and fell and found himself trapped against a bulkhead.

"Yew whut caused yer friend to fall, prob'ly die," whispered Harry.

"But we knows 'ow to git rid of 'Jonahs" like yew!" George said, thrusting his knife again at David.

David jerked sideways. George's knife grazed his shoulder, pinning his shirt to the bulkhead. George's left hand grabbed David by the throat, holding him in place, while his right hand pried the knife free. David struggled with both hands against the powerful grip holding and strangling him. George's arm prepared for a final thrust, but he abruptly pulled away.

"What's going on here?" Lieutenant Sturndale demanded.

"H'it's 'is fault, sir," said George. "Tried to pick a fight with me an 'Arry." "Pulled a knife on us," said Harry, "but George took it away."

"That's a lie!" David croaked, rubbing his bruised throat.

"Bring him along," Sturndale said. "He's been trouble ever since he came aboard."

George and Harry grabbed his arms, twisting them cruelly. Sturndale lead the way to the captain's cabin. George and Harry shoved David to the deck before angry Captain Forester.

Forester glowered down at David. "Youngman, you've been on board less than 48 hours and nothing but trouble. Why have you plagued my ship? There must be a reason! Are you in the pay of the French? Tell me plainly or I'll bare the bones on your back flogging it out of you!"

David's hoarse voice rasped, "I've been running from the will of God."

A stunned silence. Everyone knew David spoke the truth.

"For this "running" of yours, you've brought danger on all aboard this vessel, and your friend is barely alive!" Forester said.

"Everything's my fault," David said, hanging his head in shame. "The storm. The accidents. Marcus falling—all because I disobeyed and fled God's commission to preach the gospel. I deserve to thrown into the sea!"

"I'll throw you into the brig instead," said Forester, "while I determine what to do with your wretched hide! Take him away!"

Rough hands grabbed David again, yanked him to his feet and ushered him from the captain's cabin. They forced him down through the ship and shoved him into the brig. Rougher hands clasped him in irons. The guard extinguished the lamp. He slammed the door shut and locked it. David collapsed to the deck.

Alone. Miserable. Full of sorrow in the darkness. Time lost meaning. David wept for Marcus until no more tears would come. He sadly pondered each bitter step, each selfish decision. He knew God had directed every disaster following in the wake of his flight.

He thought, *God appointed a fish to swallow Jonah. Now He's appointed the Royal Navy to deal with me.*

"Then Jonah prayed unto the LORD his God out of the fish's belly."

Almighty, Merciful God, David prayed, *You control the wind and the waves. You guide the storms, both the ones at sea and the ones in the hearts of men. I've sinned by rejecting Your call to me. I've hated those You love and gave Your Son to die for and have grieved Thy Holy Spirit. I ignored clear warnings, endangered others and brought Marcus near to death. My selfishness has broken the hearts of those who love me most.*

I can't flee from Thy presence. You're with me everywhere I've gone, even in this horrible cell. O Lord, forgive my great sin. I yield to Your call. Release me from the bondage of bitterness and hate. I forgive those who slew my parents, just as I know You forgive me my trespasses through Jesus Christ. Grant me the grace to bring the light of Your gospel to people who walk in darkness.

I've brought danager upon everyone I've encountered. Have mercy on all aboard this ship. Heal Marcus and restore him to health, and heal the other crewmen as well. Please set me free from this brig and back on the way to doing Your will. Bring joy through my life to those who've sorrowed and suffered because of me.

EPILOGUE

Off Martha's Vineyard

Late December 1811

The creaking of a ship riding the waves. Now peaceful music to the ears of a young man living in harmony with his Savior and His Savior's will for his life.

"And the LORD spoke to the fish, and it vomited out Jonah upon the dry land."

Captain Forester and Lieutenant Sturndale stood together on the quarterdeck, hands clasped behind their backs. The winter sun shone in a clear blue sky. The laughing cry of gulls and the gentle slap of waves against the hull a welcome change after the terrible winter tempest. Their ship hove-to while the crew completed repairs and clean-up. Purposeful activity on the deck below replaced the storm's roar and rage.

Lieutenant Sturndale said, "Sir, have you noticed how unusually calm it's been these last three days?"

"Yes. Heavenly after that horrendous storm abated," Captain Forester replied.

"Sir, what shall we do with the man in the brig?" Sturndale asked.

"Youngman, ha-hmm. I've been pondering him and pondering him," Forester said. "I've not been much of a religious man, but it seems obvious, even to me, that the Hand of the Almighty has been in all of the trouble."

"Uncanny. Reminds me of the book of Jonah, sir, from the Old Testament," said Sturndale.

"Aye that. Eerie similarity, to be sure," Forester said. "And his injured friend, still making progress after he regained consciousness?"

"Remarkable, miraculous even!" said Sturndale. "Ship's surgeon can't account for the speed of recovery. This morning, he reports only a broken arm and a knot on the man's head to show for the fall."

"I've seen others fall from that height. None survived. Why not this fellow?"

"Trick of the wind, perhaps," Sturndale ventured, "maybe bringing him down from sheet to sheet, landing him the way he did on the longboat tarpaulin, but even that's the mercy of God, sir."

"God again. God in all, it seems," pondered Forester out loud. "Ha-hmmm. Everything going from bad to worse, and now the opposite since we threw that "Jonah" into the brig."

"If you don't mind my question, sir, shouldn't he stand before the mast and receive due punishment under the Articles of War for endangering the safety of this vessel?" Sturndale asked. "There's a strong case against him."

"There is a case," answered Forester. "But a Greater Authority than the Articles of War is involved. Beyond the Almighty's hand, I can't explain what's occurred aboard this ship. Call it the Holy Spirit or an old sailor's intuition, but I feel strongly compelled to cast this "Jonah" and those associated with him away from us as quickly as possible." He gazed out to the horizon, focusing on a distant spot. "We're off Martha's Vineyard." He paused, thinking, "Ha-hmmm." He came to a decision and issued orders. "Get under way. Set course for the island. Gather a boat's crew, the sergeant and six armed marines among them. Prepare the longboat!"

"Aye, sir!" said Sturndale.

"Bring up the prisoner," continued Forester, "along with his injured friend, and the eleven others impressed from the *Pocassett*. Restore all their belongings and anything the crew has taken." He nodded toward Martha's Vineyard. "Row them ashore. Leave them outside the island village."

"All of 'em?" Sturndale asked. "Begging your pardon, sir, but, except for the prisoner and his injured friend, we need the rest of those men in the King's Service on this ship."

"No, every last one must go!" Forester said. "A King higher even than His Britannic Majesty desires service of that man in the brig. For the sake of this vessel, and perhaps the entire Royal Navy, we must be clean of that . . . that *disobedient preacher* . . . and *ALL* associated with him. I only hope his days as a "Jonah" have come to an end. At least I can make it so, as far as this ship is concerned."

"Very well, sir;" said Sturndale, "then, good riddance, I say!"

"Ah!" Forester cautioned, "But treat them well . . . And get away swiftly, lest Providence deals with us once more!"

Sturndale saluted, "Aye, sir! The Fear of the Lord is upon us all!"

Forester returned the salute. "Amen!"

"And the word of the LORD came unto Jonah the second time, saying, 'Arise, go to Nineveh, that great city, and preach unto it the preaching I bid thee.'"

David waited beside Marcus at the water's edge where the British sailors left them. The other freed men headed down the shore, seeking help in the village a short distance away. A short time later, a wagon emerged from the town and rattled toward him on the rocky beach.

The storm of his rebellion silenced by the One who stilled the winds and waves on the Sea of Galilee. Burning hatred replaced by the warmth of God's love. David enjoyed the peace of mind for which he'd yearned. Strength of soul and a clear vision of the way ahead replaced the carnal fog of rebellion: Soon he'd bring Marcus back to Newport. He'd seek Nancy's forgiveness. With or without her in his life, he'd go on, preparing for the ministry under Pastor Newman while finishing at the University, and then . . .

David thought to himself, *And then I'll travel west. Loving a people as God loves them, as my father and mother loved them before me. By God's grace, I'll preach to them the glorious gospel of my Lord and Savior, Jesus Christ!*

"So Jonah arose, and went unto Nineveh,

according to the word of the LORD."

THE END

What About You?

The spiritual struggle of David Youngman was fiction, but the need for salvation from sin and eternal death is absolutely real, and the need for preachers of the Gospel is too. These were woven into David's story.

Have you put your personal trust in Christ alone for salvation? Has there been a time in your life when you prayed and asked Him to save your soul? That is the decision you must make through faith in the death, burial and resurrection of Jesus Christ. He loved you, sacrificing Himself and paying sin's penalty for you on the cross. He now beckons for you to come to Him. If you haven't already, please call upon the Lord today and find eternal relief from the burden of sin.

". . . Believe on the Lord Jesus Christ and thou shalt be saved."

Acts 16:31

Have you trusted in Christ and have been sensing His call on you to witness and teach others about Christ or even preach His Gospel? As David Youngman learned, God is not willing that any should perish. David also learned the truth from Romans 10:14, *"How then shall they call on Him in whom they have not believed? And how shall they believe in Him of whom they have not heard? And how shall they hear without a preacher?"* Someone must tell the lost about Jesus. Will it be you? Pray right now and surrender your heart to seek God's will in this matter.

You may contact the author by e-mail at *pilz.author@gmail.com*

About the Author

Randy Pilz is the father of five wonderful children and, at this writing, proud grandfather of three precious grandchildren.

Born and raised in Chicagoland, Randy trusted in Jesus Christ as his Savior through a community Bible study during his junior year in high school (the character Joe Anderson's testimony in Randy's novel *A Battle More Desperate* is partly based on Randy's real testimony). After salvation, the Lord led him to Bob Jones University, where he studied Bible, Speech and Drama.

Called to Christian service, Randy served as a Christian school teacher in two different schools. He later became drama director at Falls Baptist Church in Menomonee Falls, Wis. Through that ministry he began writing plays and programs as tools for local church evangelism (Some of his dramas are available through Performance Possibilities at performscripts.com).

For eleven years, Randy served as a Creative Director/Video Producer on the staff at Pensacola Christian College, producing promotional and educational videos and assisting in the production of the *Rejoice in the Lord* telecast. He later worked as an independent producer in a non-profit media ministry.

In the fall of 2016, Randy began his third "tour of duty" as a Christian school teacher, instructing Junior and Senior High Students at Mountain View Baptist School in the Birmingham, AL area.

Acknowledgments

Special thanks to the pastoral staff at Falls Baptist Church in Menomonee Falls, WI back in the late 1990's, especially Mike Ascher, who was an Assistant Pastor and in charge of an annual Christmas Eve Vespers Program. One year, he needed a short drama for that program. Without that need, the story in this book would not have been born.

I remember the moment of inspiration for the original story and picture it in my mind. I was walking from our house past a line of pine trees behind the Sports Center at Pensacola Christian College. (I was on my way across campus to work on a project while on the video production staff there. We lived on the edge of the campus in a home later removed to build the Sports Center Annex.) I don't remember what spurred the thought, but the analogy developed in my imagination how a man deep down in the brig of an enemy warship during the War of 1812 could be like Jonah inside the belly of the whale. The ship would be named *Leviathan*. Although that wasn't the Hebrew name for whale, it was an aquatic monster recorded in the Bible and a name known to many people, even if they didn't realize its Biblical origin.

I put the idea aside, and a while later Falls Baptist contacted me about any drama ideas I might have. That was the seed the Lord used in leading the writing of the original drama, "The Christmas Runaway." It must have been back in 1998, since my oldest files bear that date.

The story evolved and expanded over the past 19 years. I added characters, like Nancy, and scenes, like the one with Pastor Newman in Aunt Abigail's library, and changed a few names. I did further research into Baptist History, the Missionary Movement in the early United States, life in 19th Century Rhode Island, the Frontier Indian Wars, and the War of 1812. I began rewriting the drama and fleshing it out as a novella in order to reach a wider audience, which resulted in this book. Thank you Falls Baptist Church for setting me on that path.

Also by Randy Pilz

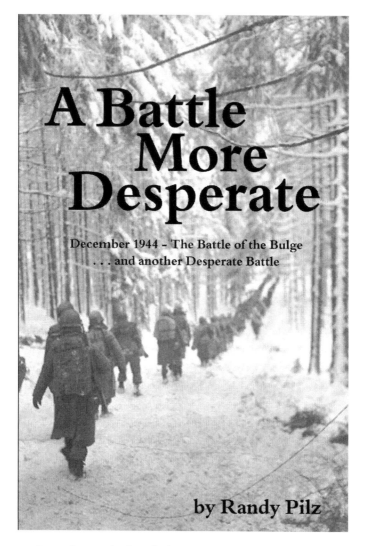

Set against the epic backdrop of the Battle of the Bulge

A parachute infantry squad in the 101st Airborne Division endure snow and suffering while surrounded by the enemy during the Siege of Bastogne. Squad members react to Joe Anderson, a new replacement, as he proves himself in and out of combat and gains their friendship and trust. In the end, the beleaguered paratroopers find victory in the battle more desperate.

Shi'mon's Journey
By Randy Pilz

A story based on the Biblical character Simon of Cyrene

Shi'mon Ben Shemu'el (Simon), a nominal Jew, lives on the coast of North Africa. He embraces the Greco-Roman world, craving commercial success; but his wife, a devout Gentile convert, yearns for a pilgrimage to the Temple in Jerusalem.

A tragic loss sends storm clouds of trouble into Shi'mon's life, confronting him with great spiritual questions. The search for answers drives him toward the pilgrimage he once spurned. Along the way, he endures opposition and intrigue from business rivals and religious extremists and faces danger from Romans and sea-raiders before ever setting foot in Judea. Once there, Shi'mon's spiritual and physical journey leads him to an unforeseen encounter with a weary and battered condemned man, a rocky hill called Golgotha and life-changing events surrounding Christ's death, burial and resurrection.

"Therefore if any man be in Christ, he is a new creature: old things are passed away; behold, all things are become new."

II Corinthians 5:17

A retelling of Dickens' short novel *A CHRISTMAS CAROL* with new characters in a new setting and a new message. Like Scrooge, Cephas Steele lives the solitary life of a miser. He considers the love, kindness and compassion represented by the Christmas season to be "buncombe." Bitter and alone on Christmas Eve, Steele broods over all he was, is and will be. Desperate for change, he realizes that "turning over a new leaf" isn't enough for saving his wretched soul. He must experience true transformation through Jesus Christ; only then will the old Steele pass away.